deliver her from evil

M.L. STEINBRUNN

Printed in the United States of America
First Printing, 2015

ISBN-13: 978-0692463277

Contents

Dedication

For my sons, Ryan and Logan. May you always find hope in the ashes of ruin and seek peace when there is turmoil. You are both brave young men, and I hope you see your courage in the pages of my stories. I am so proud of the both of you, and look forward to what you will do to make this world a better one.
With all my love,
Mom

About The Author

Author of the Redemption Series, M.L. Steinbrunn has been in love with the world of fictional characters and plot twists since she was a child. Writing short stories and reading anything she could get her hands on, it could be argued that her hobby borders on an obsession.

She works full-time as a high school educator and coach in rural Colorado where she and her husband are raising their four young children. Through education she has enjoyed guiding others on their paths and helping students build their stories.

In her free time, M.L. enjoys travelling, Amazon one-clicking, watching movies, chauffeuring her children to their one and half million activities, and people watching.

She would like to add a big thank you to everyone that has been overwhelmingly supportive of this incredibly scary and exciting journey.

Where to follow her....

www.facebook.com/mlsteinbrunn

https://twitter.com/MSteinbrunn

https://www.goodreads.com/author/show/
7383392.M_L_Steinbrunn

Acknowledgements

There are so many people that have helped to make this book possible, I appreciate you all.

My Family: My husband and children have been extremely understanding, and that has meant so much. Thank you, you guys.

My Hometown: My hometown community fully embraced this series and has been patiently waiting each new release. Even knowing that these books are romance novels, my tiny, conservative community has supported this endeavor and has encouraged me every step of the way. I truly appreciate that support.

Indie Author/Blogger Community: I have found this online literary community to be one of the most inspiring and compassionate groups. There have been so many authors and blogs that stepped up to help me, talk me off the ledge, donate, and share announcements. I appreciate every one of you. Ladies of the Indies Round Table and Indie Erogenous Zone, thank you so much for being there for me. You are the best! My street team is absolutely fantastic; you ladies are have been wonderful. You are more than a street team; you guys are a group of friends that have provided a tremendous amount of support. Thank you, girlies. There are several individuals that had a major hand in this project and deserve a special thank you. The entire team at Hot Tree Editing made this a story worth reading. My beta team: Natalie, Jenna, Con, Missy, Shauna, and Ashlee, thank you so much for taking the time to read this book and offering valuable, honest feedback. Your comments and opinions truly made this book so much better. Ari with Cover it Designs thank you for my gorgeous cover. Jovana at Unforeseen Editing did the formatting for this book and made it something beautiful. All of the blog tours and release blitz events were organized by The Hype PR. You ladies did a wonderful job, and I appreciate all of your hard work. Thank you to all of the blogs and authors that participated in the release of this book; it found its way into the hands of readers because of you.

Readers: Thank you all so much for taking a chance on me and this series. None of my efforts would have mattered if I didn't have your support. Thank you so much for allowing me the opportunity to follow this dream.

Fall 2015

Carly

"Thank you, I'll have a peppermint tea," I tell the waitress, unable to take my eyes off the empty seat next to me at our usual coffeehouse, *A Scone's Throw.*

As soon as the waitress leaves, Vivian's hand covers mine, offering me comfort. "Everything will be okay."

Vivian has always been the gentle, mothering one of our group. Today is going to be filled with many emotions, good and bad. I always knew it would be; I just didn't realize how much. Her support is helping to push me forward.

I nod with a small smile. "I know it will. Today should be a happy day. I just can't help but think about how we all got here."

Jen looks at Campbell's empty chair and exhales loudly. "It's finally time to let go and move forward. We owe it to ourselves to finally find redemption. That includes you, Carly."

"I know. Sometimes it's just hard to believe. Every day gets a little easier, a little better though," I tell them. "Today, is the final step…closure."

The waitress returns and slides our mugs of coffee and tea across the table along with our check.

"I miss her," I exhale, looking again at the empty chair. "She should be here for this. She saved my life; she made all of this possible." I struggle to hold in my tears for a friend that I want more than anything to be sitting next to me. "I owe her more than I could ever repay," I stammer, looking down at the table.

"What you're doing today would make her proud, don't forget that," Vivian says, rubbing my back.

"Did Brooks get ahold of Lakin? Is he meeting us at the courthouse with the rest of the guys?" Jen asks Vivian, attempting to change the subject. We all miss Campbell; her absence today will be deeply felt by all of us, not just myself.

Vivian moves her hand away from my back and grabs her cup to take a drink of her macchiato. "I haven't heard, but we left messages. Campbell put all of this into motion; I can't imagine he would miss it."

I nod and check the time on my phone. We are due at the courthouse in two hours and I still need to run to the house to get everyone ready. I take a final sip of my tea and throw a twenty dollar bill onto the table to cover everyone's drinks.

"I'm sorry to cut this short, girls. I need to get home and finish getting everything and everyone ready. I can only imagine the disaster zone I'll find when I get home." I stand and swing my purse onto my shoulder, and then take a deep breath preparing myself for the events that lie ahead. When I look up to offer my goodbyes, I'm met with two sets of wide eyes.

I slowly follow their stares, and emotion immediately strangles me like an albatross, forcing tears to my eyes.

"Oh, my God," I whisper, sliding back down into my seat.

Christmas Eve, 1997 (14 Years Old)

Campbell

The sparkle of the Christmas lights are almost hypnotic, and the spell they put me under makes the noise of the younger kids disappear. Each of them is scouring through the few presents that are scattered under the tree, feverishly searching for one with their name attached. As each child finds their present, they shake it in hopes of figuring out the mystery inside.

I just sit back and watch. I've already looked through the gifts, and there aren't any with my name on them. I always knew that this was part of the bargain. Being a foster kid, I should just be grateful I have a roof over my head, but I have a hard time pretending it doesn't bother me that I have nothing to unwrap. When I was younger, there would usually be something for me depending on the home I was at, but in the last few years, there has been nothing. It hurts to know there is no one to think enough of me to give me a gift at Christmas, or my birthday, or any other special time of the year. I keep thinking I'll get used to that, but I don't; it gets harder rather than easier.

Presents or not, I lucked out with the home I'm at now. I haven't been here long, just a few months, but I can tell they are the real deal. The type of foster parents who care more about the kids than the small bit of cash the state hands out to take care of us. I admit that I'm a little surprised that they didn't put anything under the tree for me, but I'm grateful to be here nonetheless.

I've been in good homes and bad, none have stuck. I get shifted around based on the needs of the system. No one has wanted to adopt me, so I bide my time, hoping someone will eventually stick. The older I get, the more impossible that probability becomes. People want the little kids. They see me, my age, and how long I've been in the system, and they all think the same thing…damaged. I don't even get the chance to show them I'm not.

I may never find a permanent home, but I'm glad that for at least awhile, I have landed in a good home, a good family. A decent place where I could stay until I'm eighteen and can create a life for myself. I would trade all the Christmas presents in the world to stay.

The ringing of the phone pulls me back to reality, and I shove down my thoughts and hopes of a family. I direct my attention back to having a nice Christmas Eve with everyone and share in the excitement of what Santa will bring all the little ones tomorrow morning.

"It's Christmas Eve; surely there is some other home for tonight. How can we do this to her today?" I hear my foster mother say into the phone. Sharon's voice is strained and defeated. The tone tells me everything I need to know—I'm leaving.

"I understand. I'll get everything ready," she adds before placing the phone back on the receiver.

I hang my head, waiting for the speech that I know is coming. I've heard it a million times. I try to gather the strength to do this all over again. Meet a new family, make new friends at a new school, all of it. Every day I fight to keep it all from hardening me. I can't let this life harden me.

I hear a few sniffles and the clearing of her throat before she calls me into the kitchen. It was just enough to break me. My throat burns and my eyes sting from the tears I can't risk shedding. I bite my lip and take a few breaths to pull it together before standing to meet my fate.

I slowly make my way into the kitchen to find Sharon sitting at the kitchen table, her gaze fixed on a small wrapped gift in her hands. She looks the same way I feel, horrible. She has been good to me the last few months and I appreciate everything. She helped me with my homework, encouraged me to go to the homecoming dance, and even offered to pay for the dress herself. I will miss her terribly.

"I know what's going on, Sharon. You can just tell me so I can pack up my bag," I say, attempting to make my voice strong, appear like I'm okay on the inside, when really I'm trying desperately to hold myself together.

"Please, Campbell, just sit down. I need to talk to you for a minute," she sighs, gesturing to the chair in front of me.

I stand still. It's not that I refuse to listen to what she has to say, it's that I'm unsure if I can emotionally bear it.

"Please," she begs again.

Giving in to her plea, I quickly nod and slide into the seat. I fold my hands on the table top and wait for my impending doom.

"I understand you are aware of what is happening, but I need you to know that we have enjoyed having you here, Campbell."

"I know. It's was nice being here, too. Thank you for taking care of me," I tell her.

I see her bottom lip tremble and I have to look away. "I'm so sorry, hun," she says, reaching for my hand. My hand recoils, avoiding her touch. I know my action hurts her, but her touch would hurt me more.

She pulls her hand back and rests it on the present. "I understand," she says, nodding. She takes a deep breath and slides the present in front of me. "I know you thought you weren't receiving any Christmas presents this year. I didn't want to put this under the tree because there needed to be an explanation with it."

I immediately meet her tear-filled eyes, which match my own.

"When you came to stay with us, I knew it wouldn't be forever, but slowly you have worked your way into our family and our hearts," she stammers. "This day was going to happen at some point; I just didn't realize how soon. This life has not been fair to you, but I see something in you that I rarely come across."

I cast my eyes down in shame. "Damage. You see me as damaged. That's why I'll never have parents again."

"No, Campbell," she says, shaking her head. "I see the exact opposite. You are a strong girl who will accomplish everything she puts her mind to. Do you know why I believe that?" she asks.

"Why?" I whisper, my head still bowed.

"Because you forgive. When things don't go as planned, you look for the good in people and situations, and you move on. You're not vengeful or apathetic. You care for people. You will make it in this world, Campbell. You just have to survive in the meantime." Sharon reaches again for my hand, but this time, I don't pull away. I let her fold her fingers around my palm, absorbing the touch of someone who has been nothing but kind to me. Someone I now have to let go.

"Do you really think so?" My voice cracks as I try to hold back my emotion.

"I do. That's why I got you this and wanted you to open it away from the others," she says, tapping a finger on the top of the small present. "Open it. Merry Christmas, Campbell."

My eyes lift to the small present before me and I take a moment to just look at the box. It has been a long time since I have been given a gift. I want to savor the moment; it might be a long time before it happens again.

The shiny red paper and white bow on top tempts me to tear into it, but I refrain. Instead, I slide my finger under the tape that holds the pristine packaging together and slowly separate it from the paper. Peeling away the paper, a white box is soon exposed. I pop off the box's lid and when I see the gift inside, the tears I had been holding back, fall freely onto the table top.

Sharon takes the necklace from the box and stands to put it around my neck. As soon as the cool metal lies against my chest, I reach up to feel the beautiful flower jewel, which hangs from a white gold chain.

"The flower is a forget-me-not, Campbell. It is supposed to symbolize remembering someone. I want you to wear this and remember your kind heart. Remember forgiveness and the beauty this life has to offer you. Forget the bad, the sadness, all of the things that could break you. Let this be a reminder that no matter where you are, you are loved." Sharon smiles through her tears and guides me to stand.

She wraps her arms around me and holds on for what feels like forever. I bury my head in her shoulder and grasp onto my new prized possession. I choke on a sob trying to tell her thank you.

"Thank you for letting my family know you and love you," she adds while she pats my back.

I nod, still unable to speak. The doorbell rings through the house and prompts me to pull away from her. "I'll go get my things," I say, turning to leave the kitchen.

"Don't forget the box," Sharon insists, picking it up and handing it to me.

I race to my room and grab my overnight bag, stuffing it with the few personal items I have. I shove my arms into my winter coat and take one final look around my simple room before walking back down the hallway to meet my caseworker.

"I'm ready," I announce when I enter the living room. All of the other children are on the couch and Sharon is kneeling down quietly talking to them; no doubt filling them in on my abrupt departure. The entire situation is very out of the ordinary, so I can only assume that it must have been an emergency placement, I only wish I wasn't the collateral damage.

When she finishes speaking to them, she stands and wraps her arm around me to walk me to the door. My caseworker, Robin, opens the door, but before I can step through the threshold, Sharon pulls me into another embrace.

"Our phone number and address is in the box," she whispers into my ear. "Use it whenever you need to."

"Thank you. For everything," I whisper back.

She releases me and I take the first step out the door; a step away from a good home. I reach for my necklace, close my eyes, and muster the strength to continue toward the unknown.

"Forget-me-nots, Cam. Remember forget-me-nots," Sharon says, encouraging me to move forward.

I squeeze the pendant in my hand and smile. *I can do this.*

Before my resolve fades, I briskly walk to the car and climb into the passenger seat. Sharon and the rest of the family stand on the porch and wave goodbye as we pull away from the curb, but I can't bring myself to say goodbye. I smile and nod to Sharon, and the smile she returns lets me know she understands.

I remain silent in the car. I figure there isn't much to say about the situation. Robin and I have been in this car more times than any kid should have to.

"I am sorry about this, Campbell," Robin tells me. "There was an emergency situation and the Foresters were the only ones who could take on the case we had. I'm sorry it meant a change in residence for you. I'm hoping we can find a permanent placement for you soon."

I turn my body to face her, squinting my eyes. "I'm calling your bluff on that one, Robin."

She looks at me stunned. "What are you talking about?"

"Please don't lie to me or sugarcoat it. I need to face the truth of my situation, so please, just tell it to me straight," I plead. "What are my chances of being adopted?"

Robin hesitates, staring at the road ahead of us. Her reluctance tells me everything I'd already figured out myself. I just need to hear the words so I can move on, so I can give up on that wish.

"Please, Robin. I need to hear it."

She finally nods. "Statistically, it's not good, Campbell. I promise I'll never give up looking, but realistically, you will age out of the system. The state will help you transition onto an adult path, but it will be without a family."

I stare out the window at the changing landscape as I listen to my young adult fate being handed down to me. I close my eyes and rest my head against the cold, frosty window. I let the chill swarm my body and numb the sadness, which threatens to overwhelm me. Robin continues to talk, rambling on about my options, but her voice fades to the background. It isn't until I feel the car stop and hear the transmission shift into park that I open my eyes to take in the sight of my new home.

"This is only temporary. We will get you settled somewhere else soon. Like I said, we were in a bit of an emergency situation and we needed to move things around quickly. I only foresee this being your home for a few weeks until we can get things settled again," Robin defends.

I step out into the frigid night, and I quickly understand her defense. The trailer park we've landed in isn't exactly a community of June Cleavers. The single-wide we are standing in front of isn't decorated in anything resembling Christmas, unless you count the festive sign that says Beware of Dog: Our German Shepard ate Santa's reindeer.

Robin notices me looking at the sign and laughs uncomfortably. "They were just approved. They passed all checks; this house will be fine," she says half-heartedly.

I hoist my bag on my shoulder and reach for the necklace draped around my neck. "I'm okay. No matter what, Robin, I'm going to make it."

Robin provides a sympathetic smile and knocks on the front door. A dog's bark cuts through the silence of the night, startling both of us. It takes a few minutes for the door to open, but when it does, my resolve diminishes and Robin's smile slightly fades.

I hold tight to my necklace, willing it to give me the strength to step through the door without tears. I'm going to need every bit of might to endure the next few weeks, or however long I'm left here.

"Forget-me-not," I mumble as I take the first step across the threshold, hoping my new gift will one day guide me home. "Forget-me-not."

Spring 2013

Carly

"Medically, there is nothing wrong with either of you. It's something we call secondary infertility," the doctor says, flipping through our medical charts.

I tune out everything from the sentence except the one word that sucker punches me in the gut…infertility. My throat burns and my vision blurs with the tears I desperately try to hold in. I can't break down at the doctor's office; I'm stronger than that. I lower my head to give myself a moment to pull myself together.

"So, are you saying we need to look at other alternatives," Jack says, as he wraps his arm around the back of my chair.

"Sometimes it's as simple as getting a correct gauge of when Carly is ovulating. So I'm going to prescribe Clomiphene, and I'd like you to get some ovulation kits to make sure we have your days correct. Hopefully, we can get this situated and you pregnant in the next few months. At that point we can reevaluate to see what our other options are if this approach is not successful."

My brain accepts his advice, but my body doesn't move to reflect it. I'm frozen like a statue, waiting for someone to break me, to push my fragile heart over the edge and smash it into tiny porcelain pieces.

Dr. Bradly tears off the prescription from his notepad and reaches across the desk to hand it to me, but I don't respond. Noticing my struggle, Jack reaches across me and takes the paper.

"Thank you, Doctor. We will be in touch," he murmurs as he folds the prescription and stands to put it in the pockets of his khakis. He then lightly grabs my arms and assists me from my seat. His touch breaks my trance and I move toward the door to get to our car as soon as possible.

I ignore the doctor's goodbyes. I disregard the receptionist when she attempts to schedule our next appointment, and I close my eyes and turn away when I see the pregnant women in the waiting room. My mission is to get to the safety of our car.

Jack's footsteps pound on the cement behind me as I rush through the parking lot. The car's security system beeps as he unlocks the door and I slide into the passenger seat. The cool leather is a shock to my system, which stirs all of the emotion I've held in. Resting my elbows on my knees, I settle my face in my palms and release the tears I refused to shed in public.

Jack climbs in the driver's seat and closes his door. "It's okay, Carly," he says, rubbing my back in an attempt to comfort me. "If we're meant to have more children, we will. There's no need to stress over this."

"What?" I ask in disbelief. "What do you mean? We have always wanted a large family. If this doesn't work, then that goes away. How can I not stress about it?"

His arm moves away from my back and he grips the steering wheel tightly, closing his eyes. "Car," he exhales, "I have a business trip next week; we can talk more about this when I get back."

"We need to talk about this now, Jack," I insist. I begin to nervously twist my long hair around my fingers. The direction of this conversation has my stomach in knots.

"I don't think now is a good time. You're emotional. We need to let it cool down before we address the issue any further." His eyes are pleading with me to leave the topic alone, but I ignore the warning. Nothing will be different a week from now; I need to hear what he's holding back.

"No. If you have something to say, say it," I stutter.

He exhales loudly and stares out his window momentarily before finally speaking. "I'm done, Carly. No more ovulation kits, no more family planning calendars, no more scheduled sex. I'm done. We need to be happy with the family we have. If we were meant to have more children, we would have them. It's not in our future, and I'm okay with that. I think it's time you accept that, too."

I vigorously shake my head, in disbelief of what I'm hearing. He's giving up. This journey to have more children is just beginning and he's throwing in the towel. Before he can say anymore, I open the door and climb out of the car.

"Come on, Carly. Get back in the car," I hear him say as I slam the door. He reaches for his door handle to come after me, but I hold my hand up to signal him to stay where he is. Shaking my head, I mouth the words that seem to seal my fate. "Go home."

Summer 2014

Carly

"Hurry, Olivia! We need to get things put away and dinner started before your daddy gets home from his business trip," I shout over my shoulder as I walk through the living room, my arms loaded down with bags of groceries. Olivia is lagging behind, dragging a small sack behind her, most of its contents spilling across the floor.

"I'm coming, Momma," my four-year-old says merrily, stopping to pick up the cookies which have fallen out of her grocery bag. Distracted by the sugary goodness of the Oreos, she abandons her task and plops onto the floor attempting to peel open the package.

I quickly fling my bags onto the kitchen counter and race back into the living room to save my carpet from a cookie crumb disaster. "You can have one if you sit up at the table with it, but no more until after dinner. Deal?" I tell her.

"Deal," she responds. Her wide grin exposes her chocolate covered teeth from the cookie she has managed to inhale before I could get to her.

I hand her the cookie and she races to the kitchen to sit at the table to eat it. Grabbing the empty grocery sack, I travel Olivia's previous path to pick up the abandoned grocery items, like a trail of bread crumbs. Once I have her mess handled, I return to the car to grab the remainder of the groceries.

"Is Daddy bringing a present?" she asks as I begin to put the food items in the refrigerator and pantry. Everything has its perfect place. After Olivia was born I stopped working outside the home. I consider her, my husband, and this house my job, and I take it very seriously. Birthday parties are well-organized, I volunteer at Olivia's preschool, and dinner is always made on time, even if it's just Liv and me eating it. I look the part. I feel the part. I am the ideal homemaker wife, or at least I hope I am.

"I don't know, Liv. You'll just have to wait and see," I tell her with a smile.

She and I both know we don't have to think about it too hard. Jack always brings home gifts for the two of us when he goes on business trips. He's been working on setting up a branch office in New York for his brokerage firm and has spent a great deal of time there. The trips have gotten more frequent and for longer amounts of time. I know it bothers him, so, to make up for his absenteeism at home, he showers us with gifts when he returns.

We have missed him, but Liv and I make do. I'm just thankful for the job he has; it provides a way for me to stay home with our daughter, and, hopefully at some point, we will finally get pregnant again or I'll talk Jack into adopting. So, sacrificing some of our time with him is a fair tradeoff for me.

Olivia jumps down from her chair and I grab a washrag and begin wiping down the table Olivia has vacated, her cookie crumbs covering the top. "Drink, Momma," she says, walking to the fridge, expecting me to follow and comply with her demand.

I rinse the rag in the sink and fold it nicely to dry and then follow her to the refrigerator. "Just a little milk, and then you can go color while I fix dinner."

She nods and I pour her a small glass of milk into a pink cup.

"No!" she shouts, just as the liquid hits the bottom of the plastic cup. "My purple one."

I halt the flow of milk because I know exactly where this is going. "I already have milk in the pink one. This is fine, Liv."

Olivia lets her body go limp and falls to the floor pretending to cry. "I need a drink, Momma. I need my purple cup."

"Oh my goodness, girl. The pink one is just as good as the purple one," I say, rolling my eyes.

"Purple," she cries.

"Olivia," I say a little more sternly. "Don't you–"

"Purple," she says in a monotone voice, cutting me off, her body sprawled out on the wood floor.

I turn and open the cupboard once more to grab her favorite purple plastic cup and pour milk into it. "Get up, young lady," I say as I put the milk back into the fridge.

She hops up and begins to swipe the cup from my hand, but I pull it out of her reach. "That was not okay, Olivia. Next time I see a fit like that, I will walk out of this kitchen and leave you on that floor. You got it?" I ask.

Her eyes cast down and she slowly nods her head in understanding.

"Now drink your milk and head to the playroom to color for a bit until dinner's ready."

Just as I hand it to her, the phone begins to ring and I race to the living room to answer it before the machine picks up. Leaving Olivia with her cup is a huge risk. I will more than likely find it empty or spilled in the playroom. I have little faith it will actually make it into the sink, but the call could be Jack, so I accept the risk.

"Hello," I pant into the receiver, leaning against the arm of the couch.

"Hi, this is Judy with Dr. Banks office, is Mr. Carrington available?"

My brow scrunches together in confusion, our family doctor is Dr. Perry and we haven't been to the doctor in several months. "Mr. Carrington is out of town on business. This is his wife; is there something I can assist you with?" I tell her.

"Let me just check the file to make sure you are listed as a person we can release medical information to." She then places me on hold and I feel a ball of nerves knot in my stomach. I can't think of a reason why Jack would go to the doctor and not at least let me know. I feel uneasy about the possibilities. Is he sick and afraid to tell me? My mind swims with horrific outcomes of brain tumors or early onset Alzheimer's when Judy's voice pulls me out of my anxiety.

"Ma'am, we do have you listed as an emergency contact. I just had a few questions regarding the billing of your husband's procedure."

My heart races and my brain replays any moments with Jack over the last few months that would indicate a procedure. Stiches, pain, anything that would clue me in, but I come up short-handed.

"Which procedure would that be?" I inquire.

"Mrs. Carrington, he has only used our office for one. A vasectomy," she answers casually.

My immediate reaction is to laugh. "Thank you for the call, Judy, but I think you have the files mixed-up. My husband hasn't had a vasectomy. In fact, we have been trying to get pregnant."

"Oh my! I'm so sorry. Can you please verify his name and birthday and I can double-check the file?"

"Of course. Jack Carrington and his birthday is June 4, 1986." I give her the information she is requesting, but there is an edge of agitation in my voice at how they can be so unprofessional and unorganized with personal information. How could they possibly make this big of a mistake with a person's chart?

"That is correct. I have this phone number listed as a secondary phone number. Can you please tell me the primary address that is listed?"

"805 Sunridge Road Westminster, Colorado," I answer.

"All right, there is our issue. I have a New York address listed as the primary. I'm so sorry to bother you, ma'am. I will continue to call the primary number listed and get this situated."

Buzzers go off in my head. New York. Could Jack really have done this and used his work office for correspondence?

"Wait," I tell her before she hangs up on me. "My husband works most days in New York right now on business. The address would be 1100 West 52nd Street, New York. Is that what's listed?"

I hold back my tears and hang onto the tiny sliver of hope that this is just a misunderstanding. When I hear her confirm the address, everything fades out. Gripping the phone, I slide down the couch onto the floor. My cries break through the silence and I immediately attempt to stifle my sobs.

"Ma'am, are you still there?" I hear Judy ask. "Ma'am, are you okay?"

I clear my throat, take a deep breath, and gather the strength to respond. "I'm here. Sorry. It seems the file is my husband's. Please go ahead with whatever you need to ask to get the situation corrected."

"Well, we billed the insurance company for the procedure, but the deductible has not been met for the year, and the insurance is placing the entire procedure toward the deductible. We attempted to bill at the address listed, but the bills have been returned. We have been trying to get ahold of him for payment and a current address to send the bill."

My breathing has finally calmed, but instead of the sadness I thought would overtake me, rage is the only feeling I'm consumed with. Rage for everything he has secretly taken away from me, from our family. I had a feeling something was off with Jack. I even mentioned it to Jen at Vivian's baby shower, but I never would have imagined he would have done something like this.

"Please use this Colorado address for the bill. I will see to it that it gets paid," I tell her before hanging up the phone.

My body is motionless, but the wheels turn in my head as I desperately try to put the pieces together. If he had this done in New York, it's entirely possible I wouldn't have known about it. He's been gone for weeks at a time, and with the stress of the job and the issues we've been having getting pregnant, we haven't been intimate much. I jog through my mental calendar, and 'very little sex' is putting it lightly. We haven't had sex in months. I have tried to instigate, but he always had some excuse as to why he wasn't in the mood. Since when is a man not in the mood? Now it makes sense.

He's hiding things from me.

Catching my breath and my bearings, I call the only person I can think of who would know what to do without completely going rogue.

I call Campbell.

After hysterically explaining my discovery, she not only talks me off the ledge, but insists I stay quiet about it with Jack. As nicely as she can, she infers there is probably a lot more that Jack is keeping from me, and to really find out, I have to pull myself together. I agree to meet her tomorrow while Jack is at work to figure out the details and plan out what she calls an inquisition intervention.

I hear the garage door opening as I'm hanging up the phone with her, so I rush to the kitchen to pull something together for dinner. Usually, I would have it finished and laid out pristinely on the table by now.

Not today.

In the last hour, my life has been put on pause while my brain rewinds every conversation Jack and I have had, every interaction between us is replayed in an attempt to figure out what has happened. I know things have been off, but this still feels like a boulder-sized curveball.

My back is turned away from the door, but I can hear every movement as Jack enters the house. Even though it feels like my senses are heightened beyond measure, his routine is so predictable I could describe what he will do before he does it. Briefcase and coat on the bench in the entry, shoes are kicked off underneath. They are things I routinely have to put away for him.

"Hey, hun. How are my girls doing?" Jack says wrapping his arms around my waist and kissing my cheek. I fight my instinct to peel his hands off me and confront him. I remember what Cam told me though, and plaster a fake smile on my face and relax my tense muscles.

"We are good. Liv is in the playroom coloring. We just got home not too long ago from grocery shopping, so we are running a little behind."

"Dinner in like an hour then?" he asks.

"I'm making shrimp scampi, so it will be more like thirty minutes. I just need time for the noodles to soften."

He smiles, grabs a bag with presents no doubt, and leaves the kitchen in search of Olivia. When I hear squeals and laughter, my gift suspicions are confirmed.

"You're quiet tonight; did you have a rough day?" Jack asks as he breaks apart a piece of buttery French bread and shoves it into his lying mouth.

Am I quiet? You bet. I've only said a few words and they have mainly been directed at Olivia. I don't really have anything I want to say to Jack. No, I take that back. I have a lot to say to Jack; I'm just not ready to say it. If he really did go behind my back and have this procedure done without discussing it with me, I haven't figured out how to process that.

"Just busy, that's all," I lie. "I put some calls into some adoption agencies and to the county's child services department." I add just as he puts another mouthful in. I made no such calls, but I want to see his reaction. His choking on a messy swirl of noodles and sauce, is the exact reaction I was expecting.

"I thought we already went over this, babe?" he says once he catches his breath. "We were going to keep things the way they are."

"I don't remember coming to any kind of agreement. I wanted to explore our options a bit more." I take a slow sip of my white wine and slide the goblet back onto the table. "If you would rather, we can do another round of testing on both of us to give that route another try."

His eyes widen slightly, but he recovers quickly. I saw it though. The lie was there in his eyes. I've known this man a long time, and while I've been pretty blind at times, I'm not this time. I see what my heart couldn't believe. He's not the man I married. Whatever else he's hiding, I don't know, but at least now I can believe he is keeping me in the dark. What he doesn't know, though, is I'm going to try like hell to find the light...find the whole truth.

Campbell

"Is Carly all right?" Lakin asks as he opens the car door of his Beamer for me. The warm breeze attacks the ruffles on my silky shirt and sends them flapping in the wind. I would usually be annoyed, but my tight, black pencil skirt is almost stifling, so I actually appreciate the breeze, warm or otherwise.

"It's not going to be pretty. This has train wreck written all over it," I answer. We move briskly across the parking lot, my patent leather stilettoes clicking on the pavement. Lakin agreed to attend a show downtown tonight to scout out an up-and-coming band. I have no problem watching these shows alone, but Lakin insisted we hang out, so here he is. While I contended this is merely a friendly evening out, Lakin is hell-bent that at some point I will refer to it as he does...a date.

"That bad? Like call for Jen-type reinforcements, bad?" He jests, but I know exactly what Jen would do to Jack if my suspicions of him are correct. No one wants assault or harassment or any other buffet of felony charges that Jen would get us. So for now, Jen will be kept in the dark.

I offer a tight-lipped smile as he opens the door to the bar for me and we are immediately ushered to VIP seating. He orders a drink and I, of course, request my usual, ice water. I say nothing more until the server returns with our drinks and we won't be interrupted.

We both take a large gulp of our refreshments. While mine is cold and soothes my thirst, cooling me down from the tight clothes and burning heat outside, Lakin's provides a sour look that only warm alcohol induces when it burns your throat. No thanks, I'm happy with my water.

"I think when we uncover what's really been going on, it's going to get nasty," I tell him as we set our glasses back onto the table top. I explain everything Carly told me on the phone, about the doctor's visit and procedure he has hidden from her, the numerous business trips back east over the last several months, and their argument over having more children. He listens intently, nodding and scowling with each new fact presented. When I finally finish my rundown, he just sits quietly for a second before taking another swig of his scotch.

"He's cheating," he blurts out after his pregnant pause.

My brows scrunch together, dissatisfied with his revelation. I know he's probably right, but I also know Carly would struggle to believe in that possibility. What her life would look like without Jack is scary for her. I love her dearly, but her strength comes from her big heart not from some protective outer shell. She's not a 'pull her up by her bootstrap' kind of girl. The big girl panties she wears daily are on because of her faith in her marriage, and if that's gone, I'm concerned about what a post-Jack life would look like for her. Because of this, it would take something of apocalyptic proportions for Carly to leave him. If Lakin's suggestion is true, Carly's world has just ended.

"Don't even pretend, Cam that this scenario isn't what played out in your head, too. He had this procedure done to protect himself from getting Carly or the mistress pregnant. He just got sloppy in his cover-up."

"Damn it, Lakin. I know that's what I thought, but for her sake, I'm hoping like hell it's not true."

"I get it. I really do. But if you're asking me as a man what the obvious answer is, that's it."

I can feel my pale face flush with anger as my temper flares. Why would cheating for a man be the obvious answer? All men cheat, and somehow that is okay and acceptable? If that's what Lakin is implying, then I not only call bullshit, but it provides a big piece to the Lakin puzzle as to why I have yet to date him.

Noticing my disapproval, he immediately backpedals. "I didn't say all men do that, nor am I suggesting it's okay. Cheating is never acceptable, Cam. Even I, man-slut of the universe, understand that. However, and this is a big however, if you ask me to call it like I see it, my money would go with him having some pretty little co-worker situated in an apartment in New York."

I nod and slide his scotch across the table, bringing it to my lips. It burns instantly and I choke. Lakin immediately stands and moves around the table to sit in the booth next me and begins to pat my back.

"Yeah, that didn't make me feel better about this shit situation at all," I gasp once I finally catch my breath.

"You really thought it would?" he laughs, handing me my water to calm my throbbing throat.

"Well, I was out of ideas." Lakin's hand hasn't moved from my back and I become acutely aware of the small circles he's lightly rubbing up and down my spine.

It feels surprisingly nice.

I don't normally like being touched. I'm not a hugger, but Lakin's hands on me feel entirely natural…like they always should have been there. I look straight ahead at the stage before us, trying to disregard the feelings sweeping over me.

"I know a guy we use at the company sometimes when we want to look into the competition. I'll give him a call and have him tail Jack," he says reassuringly. "Hopefully, we are looking too much into this, but if not, this guy will find out. Make sure she doesn't do anything differently until we can get proof one way or the other."

My head quickly turns, my eyes meeting his. "You would do that?" I say almost breathlessly.

He brings his free hand up to my face and lightly feathers the back of his knuckles along my cheekbones. "When are you going to figure out that I would do whatever you need me to?" he says, leaning into me and whispering into my ear. His warm breath on my neck sends chills down my body. The sensation is deliciously foreign.

Lakin slides his face away from mine, capturing my line of sight and holding my gaze. It feels like my heart is going to pound out of my chest. We both are breathing heavy, our exhaled air tangling in a way that only further heightens my pheromone intoxication when I inhale.

Just when I think our lips might touch and this tension I'm feeling can lessen, the lights dim and the strum of an electric guitar interrupts the dull hum of the socializing patrons. The music of the band we came to see invades my senses, and the connection with Lakin breaks as I scoot away to focus on scouting the band.

He doesn't return to his side of the booth, though. Instead, he remains within inches of me. I can feel his body heat and, every few minutes, I slide my eyes in his direction to catch him staring at me.

It puts me on edge, and I'm not sure what to do with it. Usually, when a band is on the stage, I zone in. I can dismiss everything around me and absorb myself into the notes of the music. Music is my drug of choice. Getting lost in the sound is how I coped with everything growing up, and now it's something I crave. It allows me a break from feeling, a break from thinking. I don't have to dwell on the intimate relationships I don't have or never pursued. I don't have to think about the family I don't have.

But with Lakin in close proximity, I'm distracted. He is distracting. As much as I would like to lean in and allow his arms to wrap around me, I can't. I refuse to do a committed relationship, and I know if I played with Lakin, we would be playing for keeps.

He is the brother-in-law of one of my dearest friends, Vivian. Not only do I love her, but I care for her husband, Brooks, just as much. Call it what you will, a hornet's nest, a dead end, or a massive pile of dog shit waiting to be stepped in. A relationship with Lakin could ruin all of my other personal attachments. And I love my patent leather stilettos too much to step into that shit.

So, I keep things friendly, or at least I've tried to.

I'm starting to get the feeling Lakin won't accept the brush off much longer. There is only one way to squash our mutual feelings...pretend like he means nothing to me. I only wish it wouldn't hurt both of us in the process. Staying true to the plan, I spend the rest of the evening, diverting all of my attention away from Lakin and to the band we came to see.

Lakin

Campbell has been friendly but I know she's avoiding me; she has kept me at a safe distance since the concert, and I'm pissed that I can't invade past the safe zone. She has been giving me the vibe that if I didn't have information about Jack, then meeting was unnecessary. I would like nothing more than to prove her wrong though…wiggle my way into her life so she has no choice but to give me the time of day.

Spending the evening together at Brooks and Vivian's isn't exactly what I had in mind though.

If I weren't related to these people, I wouldn't be here. This evening only promises uncomfortable conversation, the yearning for a woman who refuses to take our friendship to another level, and the delivery of news that will turn someone's world upside down. Damn it all to hell, Brooks better offer the good alcohol.

I usually enjoy coming to my brother's house. Vivian is always planning family dinners and, most times, all of Vivian's girlfriends and I are invited. My time there offers a little taste of family life without the commitment of it. I love my nieces and nephews, but I'm blissfully content with my uncle status. Seeing them isn't what has me in a sour mood, though.

No, it's their other dinner guest who has me nervous and not feeling quiet myself. Campbell is the cause.

I met her, this gorgeous, intriguing woman, last year when Vivian and Brooks got engaged. I have, of course, dated other women, just as I'm sure she has dated other men since, but I can't help but want her—only her. We have become close friends, enjoying each other's company frequently; however, that's where it ends.

I want more and she has halted me in my tracks.

Unrequited love, it's a bitch.

Here I am pining away for a woman who has forever friend-zoned me. How I got there, I don't know, but I'd pay any price for a one-way ticket out. I'm pretty sure I'm forever cursed to love this woman.

The gravel of Brooks' driveway cracks under my tires as I pull up to their house. Bikes and scooters, tee-ball stands, and basketballs litter the front grass; all signs of an approaching summer vacation.

I park next to Campbell's car and throw the folder of information she needed into a backpack. I'm pissed, and I know she will be as well, at what that folder contains. I can't help but think Jack is hiding more than just what I've uncovered; I don't trust him. I just can't figure out his angle, but without a doubt, he has more cards than what he's showing.

As soon as the car is shut off and the air conditioning ceases, the heat of early summer attacks me. I showered at the gym, but if I don't run to the house, the sweltering temperature will void any hygienic courtesy I may have intended. Ball sweat and ass rot is what initially comes to mind, neither of which will help me to win Campbell over.

With my backpack over my shoulder, I run to the door and knock as I enter the house.

"Hey guys! I'm here," I shout over the noise of children I'm met with upon my entry. There is no such thing as quiet in this house. Another reason I'm happy being just Uncle Lakin.

"We're in the kitchen," Vivian announces. I follow the adult voices and laughter to the back part of the house, giving hugs and kisses to the kids with each step.

"What's in the bag? Gifts for us?" Grace asks, pulling on my backpack.

"Not this time, baby girl," I say continuing my stride. "It's a present for Aunt Campbell."

"Lakin has a girlfriend. Lakin has girlfriend," Blake and Emma sing together.

I pin them with my eyes, willing them to hush as we enter the kitchen together. "Dude, you disappoint me," I tell Blake. "Bros before hoes, my man."

The kids giggle, but Vivian perks up at my choice of words, and now it's my turn for the facial scolding. "Sorry, Viv," I offer with my boyish charm and smile.

Brooks walks around the kitchen island and offers me a beer. "Looks like you could use this, little brother, especially now that you've come under the radar of the PG patrol," he chuckles.

"Thank you," I say, gripping the beer into my hand and taking a long pull. The chill from the honey-brown goodness cools me down, and I savor that first gulp of the liquid gold. "And you're an ass," I add once I take the beer from my lips.

"So what is this about a girlfriend?" Campbell asks as she enters the kitchen from an extended hallway.

I don't even register the words she's saying; I'm too transfixed on the beauty before me. Her dark hair is wrapped into these curled swirls pinned on top of her head, which looks like something out of a 1940s pinup calendar. Her barely-there summer dress, has my hands twitching with the need to touch the delicate skin that's exposed. In the back of my mind, I'm silently wishing we move our dinner outside in the hopes a breeze might catch her skirt just right.

Fuck, I need to get my creeper status under control.

"It's nothing. They were just wondering about the backpack. These are the shirts you had me order for you."

She gives me a look of confusion as I place the bag in her hands. "You know," I encourage with a nod and a sideways glance, "the shirts you ordered."

"Oh, I totally forgot about those. Thank you," she says, playing along.

I don't know if she wants Brooks and Vivian to know about the contents, but I figure that isn't my decision to make, no matter how great it would make the dinner conversation.

She accepts the bag and scurries off to put it next to her purse. I can't help but watch her leave the room, admiring the view. When she's out of sight, I turn my attention back to my drink and notice Brooks watching me closely.

"What?" I ask innocently.

"No," he says adamantly. "I know what you're thinking, and the answers is no."

"And just what am I thinking, big brother?" I say defiantly as I take a seat on a bar stool at their kitchen island. I know how Brooks has had a soft spot for Campbell since college. They remained close even after he and Vivian broke up all those years ago. Brooks sees her as a sister, and treats her as such, no one is or will ever be good enough for her.

"You play dumb, Lakin. I know how you are, and she's is off limits," he says matter-of-factly before taking a drink of his beer.

"Who's off limits?" Campbell asks, returning from the living room.

"You are," Grace interrupts, dancing through the kitchen. "Daddy said that Uncle Lakin isn't allowed to like you."

Bam! Just like that, Grace drops a big-ass white elephant in the middle of the room, and prances out of the kitchen like the elephant isn't smothering me to death.

Campbell looks to Brooks, who doesn't seem the least bit fazed that his daughter just made my evening awkward and uncomfortable. Her brows pull together, but I can't read whether she's upset that Brooks has forbidden a relationship with me or at the thought of actually having a relationship with me. Either way, it's not looking good for me.

"I didn't realize I had given you authority over my love life," Campbell says. She has a smile on her face, but I get the feeling she is deflecting, not wanting to make a big issue out of his demand.

Fuck yeah, Cam. Tell him to go pound sand. If we want to date, fuck like bunnies, make a million babies, that's our call, not his. I'm mentally cheering her on as Brooks silently contemplates the entire situation.

He finally places his beer on the counter and exhales loudly. "Cam, you know I love you and want the best for you. A romance between you and Lakin would go south quickly and could make a lot of relationships tense. For all involved, I don't think it's a good idea."

It's like they are not even acknowledging I'm sitting here listening to them discuss how I'm a poor romantic choice. Awesome with a capital A.

I move my lips, preparing my voice to defend myself, when Cam speaks over me and anything I had to say instantly dissipates.

"Lakin and I are just friends, Brooks," she explains. "We enjoy each other's company and hang out a lot, but we are only friends."

I sense a tinge of regret, maybe even sadness in her voice, but as soon as I think it's there, it's gone again. I silently beg for someone, something to save me, save the possibility of a relationship with Campbell, but no rescue arrives.

With nothing left to say, I give a nod of finality, gather my beer, hop off the stool, and head outside to be alone to drown in my loss. Not only did that elephant suffocate me, but Cam leashed it up and trampled me with it.

Carly

My meeting with Campbell was supposed to take place over a week and a half ago. Instead, she told me to carry on with life as usual and she would meet me when she had news. As easy as that would sound, those two days Jack was home before he left for another business trip were the most excruciating forty-eight hours of my life. I wanted to corner him and ask every question I had swirling in my head. Somehow I knew though, if I really wanted to know the truth about what was going on, I needed to take Campbell's advice and wait it out. Wait for what? I don't know. I'm almost scared to find out.

So, when the text came through this morning that Campbell had information and she would be coming over, I wanted to throw up. Coming here to deliver the blow meant something bad. So I refused the house call; instead, opting for a public meeting at the coffee shop we frequent weekly, *A Scone's Throw*. I knew if I was in public, I could hold myself together a little better than within the walls of my house. Whether it's warranted or not, I refuse to cry in public.

I drop Olivia off at preschool and make it to the coffee shop before Campbell. I take a seat at our usual table in the back with my chamomile tea and settle into the comfort of my surroundings; it may be the only solace I'll find today. Now as I wait, I let my mind drift to the days when Jack and I first started dating.

I had just gotten a job at a spa working as an esthetician, and when I was leaving work one afternoon, he was dropping off items at the dry cleaners next door. When I first saw him in his crisp business suit, I couldn't help but stare at him. He looked so charming and put together. His dark wavy hair was begging to be pulled, and even though it was late afternoon, he looked freshly shaved. When he caught me looking at him, he winked at me. Yeah, there is the charming part. I was so embarrassed about being caught, I rushed to my car as quickly as I could. I tripped over the curb and my purse scattered across the parking lot. He walked over to help me pick everything up, but I managed to get it all stuffed back into my purse and to my car before he made it to me. It wasn't until the next day at work that I realized I hadn't picked up everything.

I hadn't planned on telling the ladies I worked with about the encounter, but I was met with a million questions when I entered the spa the next day. They swarmed me like a flock of seagulls, pecking at me for information; it wasn't until I reached my work area that I understood why. My wallet and a bouquet of flowers were on my station waiting for me. No note, just flowers. I assumed it was the guy I was caught gawking at in front of the dry cleaners, or at least I hoped it was.

Every Tuesday for a month I would receive the same bouquet of flowers, calla lilies. Then on the last Tuesday of that month, flowers arrived but this time there was a note.

I'M DUE TO DROP OFF MY DRY CLEANING. HOW ABOUT A DO-OVER?

-DIRTY LAUNDRY

Now I knew exactly who had been sending the flowers…dry cleaning guy. He was going to be out front at four p.m. when I got off work. The excitement of it had my stomach twisted in knots. The girls tried to doll me up at the end of the day, curling my long brown hair and applying a shimmery lip gloss, which they promised made my lips kissable. I wasn't sure I even approved; this guy could be a total creeper. Who sends a stranger flowers for a month? Ted Bundy types, that's who.

I swallowed down my nerves and pushed the front door of the spa open to see him waiting for me. Calla lilies in hand and a huge grin on his gorgeous face, the situation was inviting…he was inviting. Instead of running this time, I smiled back and let fate take me the rest of the way.

"You sure about this?" Campbell asks as she slides into her chair next to me, pulling me from my daydream. I didn't hear her approach the table, nor did I see or hear Vivian and Jen take their places around the table. Now I'm wishing I had agreed to let them come to my house. Their presence only confirms my worst thoughts. Campbell is gripping a large manila envelope, inside of which are the answers I seek, no doubt both a blessing as well as the boogeyman ready to swallow me whole. "We can leave and go back to your house. We don't have to do this here," she adds.

She lays the envelope on the table top and I slowly reach for it to slide it closer to me. Jen quickly intervenes and takes it into her hands. "I know my usual response would be to string him up by his ballsack," Jen says confidently, "but I need you to know, no matter what is in this envelope, we are here for you. We will do whatever you ask of us, even if it means walking away and pretending we never saw what is in this package."

There is no anger in her voice, no vengeance, just sadness. Just pity. I struggle to hold my emotions back. My eyes burn with unshed tears for a marriage I may have lost. So instead of risking the release of the sob threatening to explode from my throat, I give her a curt nod. It must suffice because she glides the package to me.

It's amazing how for weeks I've been yearning for this information. I have been desperate to know if Jack had in fact gone through with the surgery behind my back, and if my chance at more children is gone. Now that the moment of truth is here, I feel myself stalling, holding onto the final seconds of what I thought was a happy marriage.

My fingers work their way under the seal of the folder and peel the paper away from the glue. Reaching in, I grab the cool crisp papers and slide them out. I have no idea how Campbell got ahold of his medical chart, and I'm not sure if I even want to know, but I'm thankful nonetheless.

My eyes scan over the report that confirms everything the receptionist at the doctor's office said. He had the procedure, he's been back for his follow-up lab work, and the surgery was a success.

No more babies.

I drop the papers on the table and take a deep breath, letting the information absorb. Vivian reaches for my hand and gives it a reassuring squeeze. "Maybe you guys could look into adoption," she says, attempting to cushion the blow.

"Viv, I think his opinion on future children for our family is stated pretty clearly here," I say. My tone is a little more sarcastic than I intend and she recoils at my outburst. I latch onto her hand and hold tightly. "I'm sorry," I sigh. "This is all just overwhelming. I mean, do I really want to stay with someone who didn't think they could talk to me about something so life-altering? He made this choice without me. He didn't consider my feelings or what I wanted our family to consist of."

Vivian delicately pats my knuckles and offers a shy smile. "I understand, Car. There is no need to apologize to me."

"Here is the rest of it," Campbell whispers, pushing an iPad to me.

"There's more?" I ask incredulously. Jen and Vivian both look to Campbell with an equally concerned looked.

"I'm so sorry, Carly," she says as a tear rolls down her porcelain cheek, which she quickly bats away. "This will probably explain more than the report will. The video is ready, just hit play."

Jen and Vivian scoot closer to me to view the video, but Campbell remains across from us, already aware of what we are about to view. The knot in my stomach tightens and my hand trembles as I touch the screen to prompt the video to begin. I'm scared, but I could never have anticipated what would play out in front of me.

Vivian gasps, Jen's knuckles turn white as she balls her hands into fists, and I quietly relieve the pain in my throat with silent tears. I think shock prevents me from fully unleashing the fury that Campbell was afraid would occur by viewing this in public.

She's beautiful. Her clothes reflect professionalism and sophistication and her black hair snakes down her back in loose silky curls. Her smile is contagious and pure happiness reflects in her eyes. The charm I'm familiar with is putting that smile in place as he wraps his arms around her waist and plants a playful kiss on her neck. Jack then weaves his fingers through her ebony locks and devours her mouth. Once upon a time, he used to kiss me like that. Now another woman has claimed that kiss, that charm.

Jack's hand slides down her spine, stopping at the small of her back to protectively guide her into an apartment building. The video pauses and then cuts back to the two of them in Central Park having a picnic, snuggling up together reading a book. The final shot is of the two of them elegantly dressed, entering an upscale restaurant in New York. Her red satin gown hugs her perfectly crafted curves. Her hair is pinned in a sleek bun, which rests at the base of her neck, and her makeup is flawless. Jack looks every bit the gentleman in his tuxedo. I know better now, though; his charm is a cover for his deception. He is nothing but a snake in the grass.

"I rescind my offer," Jen immediately says when the screen fades to black. "I will have the guys looking for a hole to put the bodies in, just give me the go-ahead."

Vivian wraps her arm around me, pulling me into the momma bear hug that she's known for. "Tell us what you need. We're all here for you, Car," she murmurs.

I look to Campbell, my eyes pleading with her to intervene, and her sympathy bounces right back to me. She reaches down to her lap and brings out another envelope.

"Oh for fuck's sake," Jen announces, gaining the attention of those around us. "What else did this prick do?"

Everyone momentarily directs their attention to her, both Campbell and Vivian scowling. She says exactly what I'm thinking though, so I don't respond.

"That video was your past and present, Carly. Inside this envelope is your future," she says, placing it in my sweaty palms. "Don't look at it now, wait until you are home and have had time to let everything sink in."

I nod and lay the envelope in my lap, noticing the ragged jeans and stretched out sweater I have on as my eyes make their way back up to my friends' eyes. I mentally compare every one of my now homely features to the black-haired beauty in the video. I could never compete with such perfection. For three years I've been trapped in the mom-zone, with snot on my sleeve and hair in a ponytail. I've thought little of my appearance, because I opted to focus on our daughter, on our home, on him. Apparently, Jack focused more on his dick.

I feel the envelope under my fingers and think about what kind of future I could even have. No husband and nowhere to live, since I have no job. My prospects are dreary.

"You can't do that, Campbell," Jen demands. "That's not okay to offer up something and then not share it with the group." She extends her hand to me and motions her fingers to hand over the mystery envelope.

I grab tightly to the tiny package and slowly bring it above the table. "Don't you fucking dare," Campbell snaps, stopping my hand from going any further. My eyes snap to hers. Aware the cursing offends me, she sighs, regrouping her thoughts. "I'm sorry, girls, but this is for Carly's eyes only."

Campbell levels her eyes at me, silently demanding I put the envelope away. "I'm sure things look pretty damn scary right now, and you know we are all here for you, but what's in that package is for you only. You need to make the decision as to what path to take for yourself, without us interfering. All that letter does is lay out the options for you."

"Campbell is right," Vivian interrupts, noticing Jen's irritation at being cut out of the mix. "Carly needs to figure things out for herself, and if she needs us, we're here." Vivian nods at me, emphasizing her words so I understand I'm not going to go through this alone.

"That's bullshit," Jen huffs. "Dropping a bomb like this, handing her an envelope, and then turning her loose is pretty crappy. What kind of friend would I be if I said, 'Good luck with that lying, cheating, asshole of a husband,' and went on my way like it never happened? I'd be a shitty one."

Jen folds her arms across her chest; her bouncing leg is practically vibrating the table. She is wound tight and I know I'm the only one who can diffuse the situation. I've been silent for much of this sit-down, just absorbing the shards of information that have shredded every piece of what I thought my life was. I'm numb from the shock, but Campbell is right, I need to process everything alone.

"I appreciate you three. I know you all have my best interest at heart, but right now I need to be alone and think things through," I say, though my throat doesn't want to cooperate and I choke on the words. Vivian squeezes my hand, encouraging me to finish my speech. "Jen, if I need a mob hit or torture instruments, you'll be the first one I'll call," I add, smiling through the gathering tears. "But for right now, I need to just go home and hug my daughter."

I gather my purse and sling it onto my shoulder. It feels ten times heavier upon leaving the coffee shop than when I entered. The envelopes are like bricks emotionally weighing me down. When I stand, my friends—my sisters—stand as well and each take a turn pulling me into their arms to give me their best hug of compassion. I then leave them still standing, expressions of concern and anger fixed on their faces.

Rushing through the parking lot, I barely make it to my car before the sobs break free from my chest. I let the tears fall as I mindlessly begin to drive around the city. It isn't long before I find myself where it all started…in front of the dry cleaners where Jack and I first met.

I leave the car running and just sit, my eyes fixed on the door of the cleaners. People keep coming and going and I almost expect Jack to walk through the door. I find myself asking the question: If I had the chance to do it all over again, would I take it? Was I blissfully happy with Jack? Yes. Do I love him and the life we had together? I thought so. If anything, I'm thankful for the daughter our marriage gave me. I would do it all over again, heartache and all, if I still had Olivia on the other end.

The diamonds of my wedding ring shimmer in the sunlight and I twirl the gold band around my slim finger. Something so tiny that is so significant; something so meaningful that now carries so little meaning. I allow it to slide past my knuckle, flirting with the idea of removing it completely when I hear my phone ding from inside my purse. Opening the satchel, Campbell's envelope reveals itself, its contents taunting me. I carefully open the package and allow the contents to spill across the passenger seat: two business cards, a check for a very large sum of money, and a letter from Campbell.

> *Carly,*
>
> *I know what you're thinking, and yes, you will cash that check or I will unleash Jen. This part is not up for discussion. I know there is a lot to comprehend, and everything you thought you knew about your life seems to be over. I want you to really think about what you want for yourself and your daughter. Whatever you decide, Vivian, Jen, and I will be behind you one hundred percent. There is enough money there to help you take the first step on whichever path you decide to take.*
>
> *Things aren't always perfect, no matter how much we wish them to be or how much we pretend they are. Perfection is merely a blind eye to reality. If you accept his faults and want to repair the damage, it is up to you to begin the healing process. If your marriage is something you want to try and save, I left a business card for a marriage counselor. She comes highly recommended and the money can be used for her services.*

However, if the damage is too great, if your heart and love for a man who betrayed you is too broken, the money will help to set you on a new journey. A fresh start. You will also find a second business card; it's for the best divorce attorney in the state. His services will no doubt help you to heal as well.

We love you,

Campbell

Dropping the letter in my lap I consider my options. Could I walk away from the only man I've ever loved? Our home, our life together? Hasn't he already walked away?

I hear another buzz from my phone to see two text messages from Jack.

Jack: Ran into a few snags here in New York. I'll be gone a few more days.

Jack: Give Liv kisses for me.

I stare blankly at the phone, willing another message to come through. One that says, "I love you or I miss you. I've messed up and need to talk to you, beg for your forgiveness." That doesn't happen though.

I gather the business cards from the seat and punch in the phone number on the card. As the line rings, I put the car in drive and head in the direction of my bank. If I'm going to do this, things will need to be in order.

"Hello, how may I direct your call?" the woman on the other end politely says.

I clear my throat and speak as clearly as possible, even though the ache may strangle me. "Yes," I croak out. "I need to make an appointment; the sooner the better please."

Carly

It has taken a bit of time to prepare for this day. As much as I wanted it all to be untrue, I couldn't pretend the affair wasn't happening. Even if I confronted Jack and forgave him, even if he wanted to leave his girlfriend and work on our marriage, I don't think I could ever forget what he's done.

We are too damaged, too ruined.

While I may be able to forgive him, no amount of counseling could make me let it go. Every time things felt off, I would be wondering if we were on this same unfaithful road. Every time he was out of town, I would be uneasy and worried there was someone else on the other end of that plane ride.

I just can't. There's no way I could live the next fifty years of my life like that.

I deserve better.

I deserve the fairy tale.

At first, I felt overwhelmed at the thought of starting over. Finding a job, somewhere to live, getting a lawyer, they were all such daunting tasks. Divorce feels foreign to me, and it seems like society allows for no growing room. There is no grieving time for the loss of the relationship, no break to pull your head together, piece your life together. It's like as soon as the ink dries, you should be ready to move on.

It's been a struggle to keep my plans hidden from Jack. No matter how much I wanted to scream at him, I held it in. I knew I would cave if I let him wiggle back into my splintered heart. I wanted to be able to walk away from him standing on my own two feet, strong, and with the upper hand. So Jack came and went for two weeks, not knowing I knew his secret.

But I'm ready now.

Campbell's money afforded me a new place to live and the retainer for a good lawyer. However, when I drove to the bank on the day of my meeting with the girls, I drained half of our savings account; well, that money has helped, too. I start my new job at the salon in two days, which will provide the financial independence I've been missing for the last few years.

My family has been less than supportive of my decision. While they are upset with Jack, they think I should at least give my marriage a second chance by trying marriage counseling. Thankfully, the girls have been supportive, helping me whenever I needed them. They have never questioned my decision.

When I mentioned I didn't want Olivia at the house when the movers came for the furniture, Vivian immediately volunteered to watch her. I want this to be as smooth a transition as possible; besides, I wanted a few moments alone in the house before I have to let go of it. I thought my forever would be there. I already had Olivia's graduation party, Christmases with grandchildren, and every other major occasion planned for that house. So to walk away from my dream house, my dream life, isn't bittersweet…it's just bitter.

I walk from room to room, checking to make sure I have packed everything. The pictures on the wall jump out at me, a reminder of the life I thought I had, which turned out to be a lie. They only reaffirm that I have no intentions of ever being in this house again.

"Ma'am, the truck is loaded. Is there anything else you would like us to add before we close it up?" the mover asks as I make my way to the top of the stairs.

I walk down the stairs and take one last look around. "No, that's everything," I say. "Thank you for double checking; I'll meet you at the new residence. I'll be just a few minutes behind you."

The middle-aged man smiles a gentle, reassuring smile. He's not naïve. In his line of work, he probably comes across this often, the soon-to-be ex-wife moving out her belongings from the family home. Nonetheless, I appreciate his professionalism and compassion.

"No problem. Take your time, we'll just wait for you at the townhouse," he says before turning and leaving out the front door.

As soon as I hear the locks click shut I let out a long, refreshing exhale. I expect to feel the vibration of my breath, emotion-filled and stammering. But it's smooth and invigorating. I have no tears left to cry. How can I mourn for a man, a love, I never really had?

Gathering the DVD and documents, I carefully set the scene for Jack's arrival home. It was the best way I could think of to let Jack in on my revelation...I'm done, too.

The film of him and his girlfriend is paused on the television screen, and I leave a post-it note on the TV instructing him to push play. I almost wish I could see his face when he realizes he's been caught...almost.

On top of the DVD player, I leave behind an envelope with his name written across the front. I thought for a long time about what I wanted to put in the envelope, the final words I wanted to part ways with. A poem perhaps. Maybe a love letter or a note of what could have, would have, should have been. They all carry a touch of nicety and civility. Instead of the words of what could have been, I leave the only thing he needed to have...divorce papers.

Campbell

The stress of Carly's divorce, the band preparing for tour, Jen's wedding, and my feelings for Lakin, have all been wearing on me. I've been in need of a distraction from everything, so when Vivian asked if I wanted to help out in the afternoons at the foundation, I jumped at the chance. It would be a great way to momentarily escape my current reality. Spending time with the kids at the foundation, some of whom are living in a situation that I'm all too familiar with, is cathartic.

It also puts things into focus for me. The last thing I should be doing is bitching about my life, when these teenagers are fighting just to stay afloat of their sometimes out of control lives. Right now, it's exactly what I need.

"Hey, Viv," I say as I walk through her colorful office, which is filled with family pictures and drawings from her kids. Vivian is such a warm person; love and charisma ooze from her pores and draws people to her. She is a magnetic force, a gravity unto herself that surrounds you and forces a smile to your face. She is the sister, mother, friend everyone wishes they could have. She is our little circle's glue that holds us together, although she would never claim that. She takes care of us all in the same way a mother would, and we are all better women because of her.

Joslyn is wiggling in her bouncy seat, so I reach down and scoop her out. She immediately goes for my hair and begins pulling it. I should know better by now to have it put up when I'm around her; she is in her glasses and hair phase, in which both are too tempting not to pull or destroy. I lightly peel my strands from her tiny fingers and twist my hair out of her reach.

"Sorry," Vivian offers as she hands me a ponytail holder from her desk. "I keep plenty of these around for that exact reason. I don't know why I even bother curling my hair in the morning. It's up before noon anyways with that hair wrangler around."

She takes Joslyn out of my arms and rests her securely on her hip while I throw my hair into a messy bun. "So what's the plan for today?" I ask, tucking the loose strands into the fold of the bun. "Do we have a lot of kids signed in?"

Joslyn wiggles and kicks her chubby little legs, and Vivian switches her to the opposite hip. She tickles her thighs and then blows a raspberry into her neck causing her to giggle and squeal. Vivian wrestles to keep her in her arms and I laugh at the playfulness of the situation.

For an instant, I imagine my own mother would have done something similar when I was a child. I don't know much about her, nor do I have many memories of her, but it seems like a common thing mothers do.

Me, I have never pictured myself as a mom. It's not that I don't think I could love a child, or even do a decent job; it's the overwhelming responsibility of it that has me skittish. I can't grasp the idea of losing a child the way I lost my parents. I know I shouldn't think of those worst-case scenarios, the icky dark things that no one wants to think or speak about, but I can't help but let those thoughts settle in the back of my mind. The thought of experiencing loss and the fear I have that your love for something which consumes you so entirely could be ripped away, scares the absolute shit out of me. I would rather have nothing than lose everything.

"There are some kids in the main hall playing games and my little ones are doing crafts," Vivian says, twisting Joslyn around to face me. She steps into the hallway toward the main areas of the foundation, away from the offices. I throw my backpack on my shoulder and follow behind them. "Some of the older kids are in group counseling sessions," she adds, pointing to rooms as we pass by.

I can't help but momentarily peek in, but I don't dare stop to listen or infringe on those safe spaces. I know the importance of sharing their stories, their highs and lows, and knowing that someone not only is willing to listen but cares. When I come here, I know it will be a struggle. It's a reminder of a past I have no intention of reliving. That life has been buried. However, that reminder keeps pushing me forward.

We make our way to the main room and the noise of laughter immediately confronts me. Ping-pong balls clicking across tables, board games, kids on couches reading or doing homework together; it's a portrait of organized chaos that would bring a smile to your face if you were unaware of what lay beyond the doors for these kids. There are a wide range of backgrounds represented here: Some are in the system, some are homeless or at-risk teens, and some of these kids are just making it day to day and should be pulled into the system's web.

This place gives them all somewhere to go. A support system and structure to help them face a world that drags them along or possibly even leaves them behind.

My eyes gaze across the room, as I try to assess what group of kids I should join, or if any need help with their homework.

A loud juicy noise from Joslyn's diaper interrupts my perusal and I can't help but scrunch my nose at the attack on my senses. "Oh my, that sounded and smells ripe," I tell Vivian.

She flips her over and smells the child's pants. "Yup, she's definitely a muddy little thing. I'm going to go change her and put her down for a nap." She notices my slight apprehension and rests her hand on my shoulder. "Just mosey around, join a game. Just being here helps, Cam; don't feel like you have to do anything specific," she explains before leaving me alone in the middle of the commotion.

I nod and take a deep breath before beginning my float around the room. I've been here a few times, but it still doesn't get easier. Just because I need this interaction, doesn't mean it's easy. I wave to the few kids who I recognize from my previous visits, some even invite me to join in with whatever they are working on or playing. I smile but decline, telling them I'll be back around. I want to first check to see if anyone needs any help with homework.

Snaking my way through the masses of young teens, I find myself in the area of cozy couches and bean bag chairs. Vivian has decorated the area with fresh, energetic colors, soft fabrics, and comfortable furniture; it is alluring. It is the kind of zone that demands a good book and maybe a snuggly blanket. A person could spend hours here, relaxing with a friend or a story, and many do.

There is only one person in the area today, but I'm drawn to the area despite the numbers. She has long blonde hair, which is piled high on her head; it's the usual hairstyle in the Colorado heat. While her jean shorts and tank top appear clean, they don't exactly fit well. Her book of poetry is turned over on the arm of the couch she's lounging on, and she is mindlessly doodling on the inside of her arm.

I watch as she allows the ink to swirl around the blue veins in her arms, connecting freckles as she moves the pen. Her head is down, intently focusing on her artistic pattern when suddenly the pen halts and she looks up at me without moving her head.

"Am I in trouble or something?" she asks. "No one was over here, so I thought it would be okay to read."

I walk around the couch and her eyes slowly follow my movement. She's sizing me up...friend or foe. I don't want to put her on edge, but I obviously have. I remember the feeling. No one could be trusted until they proved otherwise, and even then, it was difficult.

I stay standing in front of her, careful not to encroach on her personal space. "No, you're fine here. I'm just walking around checking on everyone. I noticed your book of poetry, so I thought I would stop. I guess you could say I'm a fan."

She narrows her crystal blue eyes at me. "Really? Who's your favorite?"

Another test.

She's expecting me to say something obvious like Robert Frost or Henry David Thoreau because, those are easy answers, and who hasn't heard of them. No, my favorite will more than likely surprise her and may even strike a chord.

"Poe," I tell her in a slightly challenging demeanor.

She picks her book back up and doesn't even bother looking at me when she addresses me. "Poe wrote stories, not poetry. I'm only in junior high and I've even read 'Tell Tale Heart'," she says dismissively.

I pause for a second, examining her reaction to my choice, and then I laugh...loudly. The sound grabs her attention and she looks back up at me with confusion plaguing her expression. "What?" Her confidence wanes and I see the fractures in her tough exterior, her insecurities pouring out.

I sit down on the other side of the couch and fling my ankle across my knee to get comfortable. "Sorry. Edgar Allen Poe did a lot more than just dark stories that you read in middle school. Some of my favorite writing from him are his poems, many of which are a lot lighter. Loss and dark wrapped around the light of love."

The girl puts her book down once more and gives me her full attention. I notice the scribblings on her arm again but she crosses them, hiding the markings, though not in a suspicious way.

"They are just drawings. I do it when I'm bored. It's not what you're thinking," she defends when she notices me looking at her arms.

"I didn't ask and I wasn't going to pry," I tell her. "If you need to tell me anything, I figure you'll tell me."

I'm sure she gets asked the question often. I knew a girl in the group home I lived in who was a cutter. She would hide the crimson lines along her inner thighs and arms with pants and long sleeves, but living in a group situation, it was hard to hide. Finally, a therapist joined the staff who suggested she draw patterns on her skin—turn the hurt into a different kind of beautiful. If she felt the need to cut, she was supposed to draw. I never saw how it would help, the pain was the release after all, but somehow she was able to battle the urge.

"No really," she insists, holding out her arms in front of me. "I don't always have paper, and I don't want to draw on the books from the library, so I use my skin. It helps me keep my mind off of things I'd rather not think about."

I nod in acceptance of her answer. Even if she did self-harm, that wasn't something she was going to share with a complete stranger. I look at her arms one more time and see no previous scars nor any fresh markings. There is no need to push this girl to possibly confess something.

"So tell me about Poe," she asks after a long pause that has her squirming in her seat.

I turn to better face her and relax into the cushioning of the couch. "There really isn't anything to share. His work can mean a lot of things to a reader. For me, I like how even when it feels like the darkness may swallow you whole, there is always a light, a memory of how your world may not be what it seems."

She smiles and nods slowly. "I can understand that. For a long time, I refused to give up on my mom. I really believed she would eventually get her life together because she loved me enough to do it. Then when it didn't happen, I thought, maybe I would find a family to adopt me. But now that I'm at the facility and my world is what it is, I try to find the light to make it to the other side. I figure I have to love myself enough to not be a statistic."

I offer a tight smile as an image of my younger self is reflected back at me. I feel a pull to this girl that I don't even have a name for. Fifteen years ago, this would have been me sitting on this couch with my book of poetry and funky clothing. A simple girl who had just wanted a family but gave up on that dream, in hopes of just making it. My heart aches for the girl I was and the one before me.

"If I learned anything from my time in the system, it's that you have to maintain focus on the end of the tunnel. It's when you lose sight of what you want that you get lost. Sometimes there is no one but yourself to pull you back on course."

She looks gravely down at her lap and briskly nods as though I've confirmed her worst fear. It feels like I've upset her. The kids come here to escape their lives, get a break, and here I've made this poor kid feel like shit with my philosophy 101.

"Check him out though, I think you'll like his poetry," I say, standing and moving away from the couch, ready to give her some space, now that I've shit all over her day.

Her head snaps up and moves closer to the edge of her couch cushion. "You don't have to go," she says.

"I better make my way around to the others. You know, see if I can make an attempt at sentence diagraming or maybe lose a game at ping pong. I'll be around though."

"Okay," she says with a nod. "I'll be sure to grab Poe next time I'm at the library."

"You should. It was nice to meet you. I'll see you around again some time." I turn and take a few steps before she shouts back at me, prompting me to turn around.

"My name is Leah by the way," she hollers, her eyes scan the room, looking to see if anyone noticed her outburst. "I don't think I told you," she adds in more of a hushed tone.

I smile at her attempt at manners. "I'm Campbell. I hope to see you again, Leah."

Her eyes light up, a spark of hope, a flickering of light at the end of the tunnel shining back at me. Her soul is begging to be held onto, pleading for something she's lost, the same something I once lost, too.

Someone to care.

Someone to love.

Someone who won't let go.

Instead of wandering the room, I travel back down the office hallway from which I came and burst into Vivian's office. She's rocking Joslyn and before she can hush me, I ask her for something I don't think she can give me.

"I want all of the information you have on that girl, Leah, who is out in the commons area. I want case files, phone numbers to caseworkers, everything you have access to, and want it before that girl leaves here."

Her eyes widen at my abrupt demands. I don't normally demand anything of anyone, but this overwhelming feeling to help this girl, strikes a chord. Maybe somehow by helping her find a permanent home, the lost girl I once was, who still exists in my heart and in the dark recesses of my mind, will finally be laid to rest.

I don't know how, but somehow I will make things right.

Campbell

I should know by now that things don't go as planned in my world. Life has been a constant teeter-totter, so I just grip onto the handle and hope to stay on.

Vivian had nothing in her records at the foundation about Leah, only a first and last name she used to sign in at the front desk. I called around to the different social service departments and, of course, I was given no information. I should have known better. Lakin stepped in and offered to use his investigator to find out, at least, a backstory. We were supposed to be meeting to go through everything he discovered when life stepped in and put everything on hold.

My phone rang, and on the line was someone who would be calling for only one reason.

"Get here as quickly as you can. There isn't much time left," is all he said. Evan didn't need to say anything else. My focus changed instantly. Leah would have to wait; my past was calling.

I didn't tell Lakin where I was going; I just grabbed the file and left.

It took almost an hour to reach Sharon's house. I drove as quickly as I could, hoping I would make it in time.

But now, I'm sitting outside her house, the same house I left so many years ago, and I'm finding it difficult to leave my car and go in. When I got the news that her cancer was back and had metastasized, I knew this battle wouldn't go our way this time. I knew this day would come, but now that it's here, I can't bring myself to face it.

I barely remember my own mother, but Sharon has been the closest thing to a mother for most of my adult life. She helped me with the paperwork to get into college, she would be in the front row of anything I asked her to go to, and she was my biggest, and sometimes only, cheerleader. For many years, she was the only thing that resembled home for me.

Her son, Evan, peeks through the curtains, and within seconds, he's standing on the porch waiting for me to get out of my car. I swallow down my grief and exit the vehicle. As I approach, he offers a tight-lipped smile and a head bob as a greeting. He's trying to mask his pain, but his red swollen eyes and disheveled hair tell a different story.

"Thanks for coming, Cam," he chokes out when I step up onto the porch. I don't say anything; I just wrap my arms around him and squeeze all the love I have for this family into him. In the comfort of my embrace, he breaks down, sobbing into my shoulder. I can feel his hands gripping and twisting my shirt. I stand motionless, letting him grieve for his dying mother.

After his parent's divorce, he became her primary caregiver. All of the emotion that a son losing his mother feels, he had to push away in order to take care of her. He has had to be so strong through everything; I feel like I need to offer some semblance of solace to him.

He takes some staggering breaths to regain control and nods in my neck when he's ready to break contact.

"She's been asking for you," he stammers, wiping the tears from his eyes.

I cradle his cheek in my palm and nod. He closes his eyes and leans in briefly, looking for additional comfort. When I move my hand away and take a step toward the door, he reaches for my elbow to pull me back. "I think she's been waiting for you…to say goodbye."

His words incite a wave of emotion that leaves a knot in my throat, threatening to combust. Unable to release the tears, I continue on through the door and down the hall to Sharon's bedroom.

Whenever I visited this house, it always smelled like cookies or pies or whatever Sharon had baking in the oven. The smell alone was so welcoming; it made everyone, including myself, feel at home. Now the smell is gone and has been replaced with a cold, sterile feeling that makes your skin crawl.

The door is slightly ajar, and I find myself standing in the opening just watching her sleep. She's propped up against a mountain of pillows, in what looks like peaceful slumber, but I know better. This woman, who I found so much strength, in has been reduced to a version of herself that no one should have to face.

So she sleeps. Frail, tried, battered, and defeated, she sleeps.

As quietly as possible, I enter the room and slide into the chair, which sits next to the bed. I would guess it has been Evan's resting spot for these last few weeks, unable to leave his mother's side. Tentatively, I reach for her bony hand and lightly lay my head on her legs. I close my eyes and let our silence engulf me, enjoying the few peaceful moments we may never have together again.

"I am so glad you're here, Cam," she rasps, her free hand landing in my hair and stroking the tendrils. The sensation prompts me to quickly open my eyes and sit up straight.

"There isn't anywhere I would rather be, Shar," I say with a smile.

Sharon begins to adjust her blankets and the pillows surrounding her and I jump up to help her, but she holds a hand up to stop me. "I'm okay, please sit. I want to enjoy this time with you. What little time I have left, I want to feel like a mother again, instead of being mothered."

I slowly sit back down, watching her closely in case she struggles. "I need you to give me a job, Sharon. Tell me what I can do. I can't just sit here and do nothing for you," I tell her, feeling helpless to ease her pain.

Since the day I left her house, I have done nothing but try to help others the way she showed me I could through her example. My friends, who are like my family, look to me to smooth out rough situations, to help. That makes me feel worthy of their love. Being unable to do anything for Sharon, only makes that self-doubt intensify. I need my deeds to reflect my appreciation for her.

"Oh, sweetheart, you being here is what I needed," she whispers.

I smile, knowing Sharon isn't going to let me push the issue. "Thank you, Sharon."

She tilts her head in confusion. "I can fluff my own pillow, hun," she attempts to jest, but begins to cough, causing her to struggle for air. I grab the cup of water on her nightstand and bring the straw to her lips, encouraging her to drink.

I can see her relief as the cool liquid eases her dry throat. When she's finished, I place the cup back on the nightstand next to her beloved collection of poetry. The green cover is faded and worn from years of love; the pages earmarked with her selected favorites.

"I see this hasn't gone far," I say, laying my hand on the cover and running my fingers along the spine. "I always liked when you read these poems to me."

"I want you to take that with you today. I know you'll love those words inside just as much as I have," she says.

I shake my head adamantly, "No, I can't do that. These mean so much to you."

"That's how I know they will be taken care of; you know the value of those words," she adds with a faint smile. She hesitates for a second before continuing. "I need to tell you something, Cam."

My eyebrows furrow.

Tears begin to build in her eyes. "I need to apologize to you," she finally stammers.

"Apologize to me?" I question. "You have done nothing but be supportive of me, all these years, when you had no reason to be."

"That's just it, Campbell. I consider you my daughter. I have been proud of you, sad and happy for you, encouraged you, but I know I failed you."

I begin to argue, but she cuts me off. "Let me finish," she demands, her raspy voice barely able to choke out the words. "I had several years and several chances to adopt you and make bringing you into our family legal, but I never did. I was scared of that permanent commitment. I thought I wouldn't be able to do a good job being a foster parent if I took that on; I wanted to be able to help as many kids as possible. But looking back at everything, I didn't take the right path, and I'm sorry for that. I should have been your mother."

Emotion builds behind my eyes and I struggle to breathe past the constriction in my throat. "You didn't have to make it legal for me to know you care about me. I knew I belonged here," I tell her.

"Whatever the paperwork said, you belonged here," she whispers through tears as she places my hand on her heart. "You are loved, Campbell. I'm so thankful you came into my life."

I nod, unable to speak from the pain that is tearing apart my insides. I squeeze her hands, hoping she feels every ounce of admiration and gratefulness I have for her.

A weight has noticeably been lifted from her. For several minutes, we let the silence hang in the air, both of us settling into the peace of the moment. I slowly flip through the pages of her poetry book, taking note of the highlighted passages, notes in the margins, and a few of her favorites that she insisted I read at different times over the last decade and a half.

"Will you read your poem for me?" she finally asks.

I look up at her, almost surprised at her request. "Just that one? I would be happy to read some of your favorites."

"I'm getting tired, Campbell. I would like to hear it one more time. I want you to say the words one last time," she murmurs.

I turn the pages until I reach the poem she has requested and take a deep breath, staring at the words on the page. She made me read this William Wordsworth poem so many times over the years; there really is no need to actually read it. The words are burned into my memory, but I need to keep my eyes and mind distracted. As soon as the first words leave my lips, her eyes close and she relaxes into the rhythm of the poem. My voice trembles through the first few lines until I can find comfort in the words.

SHE DWELT AMONG THE UNTRODDEN WAYS

BESIDE THE SPRINGS OF DOVE,

A MAID WHOM THERE WERE NONE TO PRAISE,

AND VERY FEW TO LOVE.

A VIOLET BY A MOSSY STONE

HALF-HIDDEN FROM THE EYE!

FAIR AS A STAR, WHEN ONLY ONE

IS SHINING IN THE SKY.

SHE LIVED UNKNOWN, AND FEW COULD KNOW

WHEN LUCY CEASED TO BE;

BUT SHE IS IN HER GRAVE, AND OH,

THE DIFFERENCE TO ME!

I recite the final stanza and slowly close the book. My gaze finally rises to see Sharon, peaceful in her bed, no longer struggling to breathe....gone.

For the second time in my life, I've lost my mother. I'm just thankful that this time, I had the chance to say goodbye. A sob breaks free and I unleash the tears I have been straining to contain. Barely able to catch my breath, I grip onto the book, rest my head on her legs once again, and let my blended heart spill out.

Campbell

My mind, my heart, screamed for a distraction. I needed something to pull me away from the pain of my loss.

I will be the first to admit I've struggled with Sharon's death. I didn't tell anyone about it, and allowed Evan and I to grieve alone, together. She had all of the funeral arrangements in place; all we did was make the announcement of her passing. It was a beautiful ceremony with so many people in attendance that there was no more room in the pews at the church. Previous foster children, who now had families of their own, community members, family, all there to celebrate how valuable her life was to them.

I listened as Evan spoke about his mother and how she loved so deeply and was adored by many. I listened and wished it to be over; I wanted to walk out of the church and be able to let that part of my life go. I wanted to not miss her, not love like I had, because I faced the same pain and grief I had when my parents died.

My wish didn't come true.

So the distraction of my birthday was a diversion I gladly welcomed.

The girls planned such a nice birthday lunch for me, and I loved them for it. However, tonight has been what I have been most looking forward to. Lakin has been extremely persistent about spending time together, and I haven't been strong enough to ward him off. The exact opposite, in fact. I find myself looking forward to our time together, even if it's just as friends. I've kept my blossoming friendship with Lakin a secret, and I would love to share our relationship with the girls, but I know better. It would upset Brooks, it could make things awkward with Vivian, and it could strain those friendships. So for now, he stays a secret. Now more than ever, I need that friendship.

I wasn't surprised when he demanded we spend time together on my birthday. I cleared my evening and he commandeered the available time.

When Lakin told me what we were doing tonight, I admit I was more than excited about it. I've only been bowling once in my life, the girls took me back in college, and I was worse than terrible. Thank goodness for the bumper pads that kept my granny-throws in the lane.

As horrible as I was, I had so much fun. I love getting to do things I didn't get to as a kid. I never willingly let myself wallow in the fact I missed out. A childhood with sleepovers, birthday parties, and trips to the zoo isn't what I had. So now, as an adult, it always feels extra good to make up for those things.

As I pull into the parking lot of the bowling alley, I park in the open space next to Lakin. He sees me, steps out of the car, and hustles to my spot to open my car door. My brain becomes mush and I have trouble concentrating for a moment. Lakin is a very attractive man, young, but attractive. I've managed to box him into a certain category, one with suits and business transactions. Tonight, when he stepped out of his car, he kicked through the square I pegged him into and now he stands before me, a man after my own heart.

Faded jeans hang on his hips, paired with a vintage t-shirt, which looks like it might have actually been at Woodstock, and a pair of black Converse. He reaches out his hand to help me out of the car and smiles when he notices my own purple Chuck Taylors.

"Cool shoes," I slyly say as I take his hand. His strong grip feels nice wrapped around my fingers. I fight the urge to thread our fingers together and enjoy the idea of us as a couple.

"Shoes?" he asks dumbfounded. "I thought it would be the shirt that won you over. It took forever to find this Led Zeppelin shirt. I dressed up for your birthday." He squeezes my hand and closes the door behind me.

"Don't worry, I'm impressed by the shirt, too. You did well, Lakin," I tell him, lightly pulling my hand away from his. I feel the loss instantly and regret the decision. Without skipping a beat, he places his hand at the small of my back and leads me into the bowling alley. It feels very couple-like, even though we are not a couple. If Brooks ever found out we were even hanging out as much as we do, he would be livid with Lakin. Since that first semester at college, Brooks has always been that older brother figure to me and he would expect the same treatment from Lakin. For us to venture into the realm of dating, would throw that relationship off kilter, and Brooks wouldn't stand for it. For the sake of keeping the peace, I keep Lakin at a friendly, but appropriate, distance.

As soon as we pass through the entrance, I take a deep breath and let the stale beer and dirty shoes smell that's wafting through the breeze from the ball return fans infiltrate my nose. I find it weird how bowling alleys have a specific odor to them. Jen would be throwing a fit at being subjected to such an aroma, but it brings a smile to my face. It's the smell of people who are here to let off steam; it's the smell of families who are out for a G-rated night on the town. Tonight is no different. Laughter occasionally interrupted by the sound of pins being knocked down, echoes through the place.

We gather our rented shoes, bowling balls, nachos, and sodas before finding our open lane.

"What are you staring at?" Lakin asks, noticing how I've centered my attention on the family one lane over. The children next to us squeal excitedly every time a pin falls. The parents provide high fives and hugs to each child as they return from their bowling attempt. I can't pull my eyes away from the scene before me.

It's pure bliss. It's a family. Something I can't remember ever being a part of, nor do I foresee ever having.

"I'm just glad we came here tonight," I tell him as I finish lacing my red and brown leather bowling shoes. "Thank you for inviting me."

"I can think of a million and a half ways you can repay me," he says suggestively, wiggling his eyebrows and scooting closer to me on the bench.

"Oh my word. You're terrible," I chuckle, pushing him away from me. "Go bowl. You obviously have some pent up tension you need to let out." He lets out a bellowing laugh and stands to retrieve his bowling ball.

"I guarantee bowling isn't going to help with that."

I pick up the nachos and shovel a chip into my mouth. "Well, if you keep it up, we won't have to worry about anyone finding out about us hanging out. Brooks will let Jen neuter you, and then you can join us as one of the girls during our coffee get-togethers."

He brings his hand up in surrender and laughs. "Mercy. I give up; even I know well enough to stay clear of Jen."

Turning away from me, he slides his fingers into his bowling ball and hauls it up into position just in front of his face to line up his roll. Taking three long strides, he swings his arm back, and just as he slings it forward again to release it down the alley, I announce, "Then again, sex usually fixes most things."

Startled, Lakin's forward momentum stalls and he drops the bowling ball. It loudly crashes onto the pine floor and rolls into the gutter. It doesn't even make it halfway down the lane before the ball stops completely. He spins around to look at me, and his stunned expression quickly morphs into a scowl.

I burst out laughing. "I'm sorry, I couldn't help it," I croak out between giggles.

"That's not even fair. Mocking my weakness, have you no shame?" He plops down next to me and swipes the nachos from my hand. "You've lost your right to the nachos," he pouts.

"Oh come on now. I'm only kidding. That was funny, you have to admit." I try to cushion his souring mood and finally a small smile breaks through.

"I don't think you should ever joke about having sex with me, Cam. It's an experience that will certainly leave you with a smile, but no one will be laughing." He glides his hand across my cheek and pulls me closer to him. I can feel his breath against my neck provoking a shiver that wakes all of my senses. I feel my breath catch and I'm waiting for his next words to rescue me.

"It's your turn to bowl," he murmurs. He then pulls away and pops a sloppy chip into his mouth, a wicked grin plastered across his face.

My stalled breathing pattern is now in overdrive and I feel like I may hyperventilate. I'm not sure if I'm turned on or angry. It's entirely possible that I'm slightly both. My mind swirls as to what to say, how I should respond to recover.

"Sir? I brought your ball back," the child from the nearby lane interrupts, handing Lakin the ball. He's young, maybe six or seven, and I'm shocked he can even carry the bowling ball. "Don't worry, mister, I couldn't keep it in the lane when I first started either. I don't think I was that bad, but just keep practicing and you'll hit a pin."

I get control of my breathing, thankful for this little guy's interruption.

"Thanks, buddy, I'll keep trying," Lakin says, grasping onto the ball and shooting me an evil look. I cover my mouth to stifle the giggle that is attempting to break free.

The little boy returns to his parents and Lakin gives them a wave of appreciation, slight embarrassment written on his face.

Lakin Ryan is not used to losing or finding himself in compromising positions. He maintains control in all areas of his life, whether in the business world, when he's practicing jujitsu, or his personal life. Our friendship tests those boundaries for him, which is why he's so eager to sleep with me so he can place "us" in a familiar box. Someone to conquer and move on, which is why Brooks has put his foot down against any "us" happening.

I take a drink of my soda, allowing myself more time to collect myself, and then grab my blue bowling ball. I take my typical granny shot stance and heave the ball down the lane. It moves rather slowly, spinning and twirling between the guide arrows. Finally, when it reaches the pins, it slams into them, forcing a domino effect, which results in a strike. I whirl around and throw my arms in the air in excitement.

"Take that!" I shout. "I think I'm winning…by a lot, Mr. Ryan." I jump around in what can only be referred to as an uncoordinated attempt at a victory dance.

"You know, I would gladly lose again if it meant I got the chance to witness whatever that spectacle of movement was," he jokes.

"Jealousy is not a pretty shade on you," I jest, smiling as confidently as I can. "You only wish you could see this body move." My eyes widen at what just came out of my mouth. I was bold, it was inappropriate, and there is no way I could follow through on the invitation. I stammer to find the words to correct my blunder, but nothing comes to mind.

I feel his eyes scan over my body, carefully planning his reaction. He takes his sweet time, evaluating my body language, and I squirm under his scrutiny. I'm always calm and collected, but this man has me rattled; my insides shake and thunder from the nerves his presence provokes.

He finally places the chips on the bench and stands next to meet me on the wooden floor. My eyes search his, waiting for what, I don't know, but the weight of the air between us is strangling me. I'm struggling and only his words will rescue me.

One hand snakes around my waist and delicately pulls me to him, while the other grabs the base of my neck. He inches closer to me causing my heart to pound in my chest.

"You don't scare me, Campbell," he whispers. "You don't want to rock the boat, so you pretend this is nothing more than a friendship, but we both know that's a lie."

He kisses my cheek, slow and tender, and just when I think he might finally move his lips to mine to silence my aching misery, he pulls away from me.

"I'm here when you're ready, but until then, I'm done chasing you, Cam." He looks into my eyes, searching for a green light from me. I feel the pain in his voice as he delivers each word. He has launched the ball into my court and is waiting for me to hurl it back.

But I can't. I stand motionless, unable to say the words he wants to hear.

The silence engulfs us; the tension increasing to an unbearable degree.

"That's what I thought," he says, nodding his head, his disappointment evident. He quickly grabs his shoes and walks to the parking lot, not even stopping to return his rentals.

I bite back the tears and swallow the throbbing knot in my throat. He's right; it's a lie. I'm a liar who has sacrificed a relationship with a man I could love more than the only family I have.

I watch him walk out the door, and as soon as it closes, a renegade tear escapes. I brush it away as hastily as it fell. Taking a deep breath to gather my emotions, I slide off my rental shoes and put my Converse back on. I don't rush as I push the shoes back onto the counter nor when I walk to my car. Instead, I let the gravity of the evening, of our conversation, sink in.

I've lost Lakin.

Lakin

When I walk out of the bowling alley, I'm so pissed and so hurt that I can't think straight. I don't know where to go or who should have to pay for my misery, but I want someone to feel my wrath.

That's not correct; I know exactly who should pay for my anger...Brooks. If he had just minded his own fucking business, if he had never said anything to Campbell, we would be a couple and we would be enjoying a nice evening celebrating her birthday.

I text Brooks and tell him to meet me at the gym to blow off steam. I figure a few rounds on the mats will make me feel slightly better; I don't have many other options. Dressed and ready by the time Brooks pulls in, I bounce from one foot to the other to get the blood flowing and my body awake for the match. My hands are wrapped, I'm stretched, and I'm ready to provoke him into a dual of warriors.

Oblivious to my mood or my need to beat the shit out of him, he happily bounds across the parking lot to meet me for our bout. He's dressed in his athletic clothes, so I just give him a head bob to acknowledge he's here and wave him over to the mats.

"It's been a while, Lakin. Is there a reason for our evening workout?" he asks cheerily, but I sense the suspicion in his voice.

"Like you said, it's been a while. Besides, I needed to get out of the house." My response is clipped; I'm here to use my fists, not words.

Brooks nods. "Yeah, me too. The kids are doing a Disney movie marathon, and I just cannot watch Sleeping Beauty anymore. Vivian can handle the crew." He smiles devilishly as he stretches his legs and arms.

I barely hear his explanation as I focus on staying warm. Bouncing from side-to-side, I wait for his signal to begin. We are usually pretty evenly matched and I need to find an advantage to win. So instead of waiting for the customary handshake, as soon as he steps on the mat, I take that as the go-ahead. Lunging forward, I lift him off the mat and slam him to the ground. I instantly jump up and wait for him to recover, so I can attack again.

It temporarily knocks the wind out of him, but when he catches his breath, he shoots me a glare that shows his dissatisfaction with my unsportsmanlike conduct. As soon as his feet are solidly planted on the ground, I lunge again, pushing him until he trips and lands on the mat once again.

I hop up and he quickly follows suit. "I'm getting the feeling that this isn't a friendly workout. Mind explaining what the fuck is going on and why you are insistent on putting me in my place?" he asks.

We circle around each other, both in a fighting stance, waiting for the other to pounce. "I don't know what you mean, big brother," I say coolly. "I'm just getting rid of the stress of the day."

He stands straight up and wipes the sweat from his brow. "That's how it's going to be, huh?" he asks. I take a swing at him and he throws his forearm up to block it.

"I'll take that as a yes then," he says as he bends back down into a defensive position.

We continue to circle each other, taking turns throwing jabs or connecting roundhouse kicks. It isn't long before we are both sweaty and breathing heavily…no one a clear winner.

"You know adults talk about their problems instead of using their fists," he says between labored breaths.

"That's rich coming from the man who used to use pussy as a pain reliever," I spit out.

His eyes squint and his nostrils flare. I've struck a nerve; I knew it would, but I threw it out there anyway. The insult hangs in the air while Brooks weighs his options, fight or flight. If he's the brother I grew up with, he's going to charge, so I brace myself for the impact.

"Grow the fuck up, Lakin," he snaps. "You know, this is exactly why I told Campbell to stay away from you, when she asked about you. You're a child who has no concept of what it takes to love a woman properly."

His reference to Campbell has me seeing red. I say nothing, but my body shakes with anger. How dare he think I couldn't love her the way she should be loved? What a self-righteous asshole to put that shit on me.

After several moments of silence, he shakes his head and turns his body to walk off the mats. "That's what I thought," he mumbles.

A roar builds in my stomach, up into my chest, and rips out of my throat as I rush toward him. Hearing my bellow, he spins around and readies himself for the blow. We smash together, stumbling around the mat, each of us working to get the other in a headlock.

Our bodies slam to the ground, pain shoots through my shoulder from the landing. I let out a pained grunt, but I continue my battle.

"Get off me, you asshole!" Brooks grumbles as we roll around on the ground.

"Asshole? You don't see me sticking my nose in other people's lives and relationships. That dick move is all you, brother." I'm able to wiggle on top of him and wrap my arm around his neck.

"What in the hell are you talking about?" he chokes out.

"Campbell, you prick," I say as I squeeze as hard as I can. I know if I hold him like this for too long, he'll pass out, so when I feel him tap my elbow, I loosen my grip and let him roll flat onto the mat.

He's breathing hard to catch his breath; I can see his chest heave up and down with each inhale and exhale. I rest flat on my back and just stare at the water-stained ceiling tiles above us. My muscles feel strained, but the adrenaline rushing through my system is keeping any discomfort at bay.

"Damn it, Brooks, I like her. She makes me want to treat her properly. She makes me want what you have," I sigh.

Neither one of us looks at each other; we just lie still, letting my words sink in.

"You don't deserve her," he finally says.

"I fucking know that, Brooks," I resign. "But I want to."

"And what happens when you fuck it up? I refuse to cut either one of you out of my life."

I jump up, and Brooks slowly follows until we are both standing, squaring off once more. "Look, I get that you think of her as a little sister, man. I really do. You want to protect her because there isn't anyone else in her life to do it, but she's a grown woman. Don't you think she should be able to make her own decision about me? Why ruin it before anything has even started?"

He looks me up and down, analyzing my body language. I feel like I'm bacterial goop under a microscope and with one word he'll eradicate me. He exhales heavily and throws his hands in the air. "Fine. But if you hurt her, I'll never forgive you."

"Brooks, I don't even know if she'll want me. All I'm asking for is the opportunity to find out."

He extends his hand for me to shake. "Then go find out," he says as I reach for his hand.

I smile and he wraps his sweaty arm around my neck and tussles my hair the way he used to when we were kids. "You're an asshole, don't forget that," I tell him.

"Noted." He pushes me forward. "Now get the hell out of here."

I step off the mat and head toward the locker room to shower, but then I turn back to Brooks, who is on his way out the front door. "Hey, Brooks, we're good, right?" I holler across the gym.

He opens the glass door and stands in the entrance. He finally smiles and nods his head. "Yeah, we're good," he says before walking through the exit to his car. As soon as the door closes, I rush to the shower and wash the proof of my temper tantrum off my body. Knowing I have Brooks' approval, I can't get to Campbell fast enough.

I grab Italian takeout and a box of birthday cupcakes before rushing to Campbell's apartment. As I pull up out front, I notice there are no lights on in her apartment. It's not too terribly late. I would be surprised if she was asleep already, but I don't want to wait for another time. I need to see her now.

I race up the stairs as quickly as possible with all of the food I'm carrying. My excitement prevents me from knocking lightly; instead, I'm pounding on her front door, willing her to open it and put me out of my misery. I alternate knocking with yelling her name and asking her to open the door with no avail.

"Dude, she's obviously not home. Maybe try calling first," the man across the hall says as he opens his door in his pajamas. "We, however, are home and would appreciate it if you took the racket someplace else."

"Sorry, sir. I just wanted to make sure that if she was asleep I knocked loud enough to wake her," I explain.

"Well, I think you knocked and yelled loud enough to wake the entire floor. I'm going to go out on limb and say she just isn't home."

I reach into my grocery bag to offer a cupcake as an apology, but before I can say anything, he slams the door, leaving me once again alone in the hallway. Feeling deflated and rejected, I get a better grip on my bags and begin my pathetic, lonely march back to my apartment. I'm no longer in a rush; my evening feels anti-climactic and a letdown.

Before walking into my building, I throw away the takeout food in the trash bin on the street. I'm no longer hungry, and besides, I'm sure it's cold and stale. I keep the cupcakes though; I figure I can track Campbell down and give them to her tomorrow.

I take a deep, tired breath and push the button to take me to my loft. Closing my eyes, I run my fingers through my ragged hair and attempt to swallow my disappointment. What a shitty night.

The ding of the elevator chimes and the doors slide open prompting me to take a step toward my ride up. I slowly open my eyes and move to gain entry in to the elevator, but my body pauses and I drop the cupcakes onto the floor of the building foyer. I'm shocked at what I see and it freezes me in place.

Campbell

My mind is all over the place as I drive home. The only thing I want to do is get home and find a record to lose myself in. It's the only thing that will help me erase these feelings. I don't do loss, and Lakin will be a difficult one to get over.

I've searched every vinyl album I have and nothing seems to dull the twinge. My thoughts keeping drifting back to him, and what I've done. No solution presents itself and I can't wrap my head around how to make this better.

I'm a fixer. I fix problems for people and avoid personal attachments where I could be the collateral damage. It's a skill I mastered in the system and yet, somehow, I've found myself in the middle of a fire storm that could completely incinerate my heart. Lakin is a flame so tempting, I welcomed the burn. I wanted his permanent mark scarred across my soul, but my fear of what I might have to sacrifice held me back.

I turn off the stereo and lie down in bed. Pulling the blankets over my head, I hope the darkness and sleep will drown out the noise in my head.

It doesn't help.

I just toss and turn, my thoughts of Lakin, Brooks, and the girls pull me in a million different directions. Growing more and more frustrated, I finally rip the tangled sheets from my body and let the cool evening breeze chill my skin. Seeking some kind of relief, I grip my necklace, my fingertips tracing the metal petals of the flower. I attempt to think of what Sharon might have counseled me to do.

I think about her poem and the words she left me with. I go over in my mind what she wanted for me and the regrets she had. I flip on the bedside light and open my nightstand drawer where her book is safely tucked away. Opening it to the page with her poem for me, I slowly read the words. I repeat the final words for the poem aloud, letting the meaning wash over me.

SHE LIVED UNKNOWN, AND FEW COULD KNOW

WHEN LUCY CEASED TO BE;

BUT SHE IS IN HER GRAVE, AND OH,

THE DIFFERENCE TO ME!

Sharon's message is loud and clear.

My big ball of fear will only lead to regret. I was her Lucy…I can't allow Lakin to be mine. I quickly jump out of bed and throw on my jeans and Chucks. I don't worry about the knotted bun on top of my head or my lack of make-up; I just grab my car keys and rush to the one place I should have never left…Lakin's arms.

Standing in front of his door, the gusto of the moment is beginning to fade, and now I'm just nervous as hell. What if he's finished with me? What if he thought it's over and thinks Brooks is right that he should stay away from me? It all whirls together and muddles the thoughts in my brain, but then I wonder, what if he loves me and is just waiting for me to realize I could love him, too? Before I can talk myself out it, I knock loudly on the door of his downtown loft.

No one answers, so I knock again. Still no answer. I look down at my watch and tap the glass face. Ten is late, but not that late, especially for Lakin. I knock one last time, but when he still doesn't answer, I turn and head back to the elevator.

My confidence has flattened, my nerve gone. When the metal door opens, my shoulders slouch in defeat and I walk into the elevator. I feel stupid; this was such a bad idea. I want nothing more than to skulk home and crawl into my bed, pretend none of this happened.

Then the doors open, and there he is.

He drops a bag of pastries, the rough landing forcing the plastic lid to pop off and allows a few of the cupcakes to spill across the marble floor. He blinks a few times in disbelief.

"What are you doing here?" he finally asks.

Without a word, I move out of the elevator and bend down to clean up the spill, but he grabs my bicep and halts my movement. "Leave it, Cam. Tell me why you're here."

I can tell by the way he says it that he knows why; he just wants to hear me say the words.

"I, uh," I stammer. "I wanted to talk to you."

He steps over the bag and pushes me to the back of the elevator and pins my arms above my head. "What did you need to say, Cam?" His voice is raspy and tempting. He's daring me to bare my soul, and heaven help me, I want to reveal it all.

The doors close behind us.

The only sound is our breathing, tangling and mingling into an intoxicating passion that I no longer want to resist. His body pressed against mine feels like a peace I've never known and the sensation is overwhelmingly distracting.

"Tell me, love" he whispers into my neck.

Without hesitation, I give in to his request. "You were right; I'm a liar," I murmur.

He pulls away, perplexed by my response. He focuses every bit of his attention on my eyes, searching them for an answer. He looks as though he could swallow me whole, taking every bit of my fear, shame, sin, and lack of confidence with each delicious lick. Eluding his advances is no longer an option, nor would I want it to be.

"I want you to show me the truth," I say with a knowing smile. His understanding snaps into place with a grin before he smashes his lips onto mine. Without contemplating the consequences or the implications of our relationship, we blissfully drown into each other. His mouth and hands bring my body to life, and I attempt to match him with equal vigor.

"Hmm, excuse me, are you finished with the elevator?" I hear a gentleman ask after he clears his throat.

Lakin and I break apart and I stifle a laugh into his shoulder when I notice that not only have the elevator doors opened again on the ground floor of the lobby, but a middle-aged couple were witness to some, or possibly most, of our elevator make-out session.

"Sorry, sir. I thought I had punched the button," he says as he presses the button for his floor. "Have a lovely evening," he adds as the doors close.

Immediately we both burst out laughing. "How embarrassing," I giggle.

"Just a tad," he laughs. "At least you get to leave and save yourself from any future humiliation. I pass that guy every morning on my way to work."

The doors once again slide open and we step into the hallway to his apartment. Lakin laces his fingers with mine, kisses my knuckles, and pulls me to his front door. "I'll gladly accept every ounce of embarrassment if it means I get to kiss you again," he says before opening the door for me.

I've been to his loft several times, but it feels different now. Although we've allowed ourselves to dive into a forbidden realm, the tension is no less palpable. I'm unsure of how to proceed. I don't know how to behave around him or what to say. My insecurities heighten now that there's something different on the table for us. My hands start to get clammy and I fidget to calm my nerves, which have my stomach doing flip-flops.

Lakin notices my discomfort and pulls me to him. "Relax, it's just me. It's the same old us." He lightly lands a kiss on my temple and I melt into his arms. The anxiety evaporates and all I feel is ease.

I nod and he squeezes my hand once more.

"Now, are you hungry? I was bringing you dinner and cake for your birthday, but it ended up in the trash and all over the lobby floor. Remind me to tip the super a little extra this year for having to clean that frosting mess up," he says mindlessly as he moves into the kitchen.

He opens the fridge and rattles off a few of the options he has, which isn't much. Actually, it's rather pathetic what his fridge and cupboards contain. "I thought you were Mr. Kung Fu? Aren't you supposed to have a well-stocked kitchen with plenty of protein and carbs for training days or something?" I tease.

"Hey now. You ladies have granny-panty laundry day; I'm allowed to have take-out grocery day," he defends, pulling a stack of take-out menus from a drawer and throwing them on the granite countertop.

"Anything that delivers is fine with me; I'm starving." My stomach grumbles in confirmation and Lakin laughs.

"The sooner the better, I suppose as well."

He snatches his cell phone from the pocket of his athletic jacket and dials the number to a pizza place nearby. I take the opportunity to stroll around his apartment and evaluate his place a little more in depth than I cared to before.

I'm surprised at how comfortable his apartment is. It's sleek and modern, but not so minimal that it feels cold. It's the exact opposite, actually. The black and white photography of historical buildings and parks strategically mixed in with family photos give off an element of sophistication while still maintaining that homey allure. The splashes of color against a grey base color scheme screams interior decorator.

It doesn't shock me that he would spend the money or time on professional help with his space. Lakin is a man who enjoys the finer things in life and has the bank account to indulge those compulsions. Designer suits, prestigious universities, country clubs, and rubbing shoulders with industry leaders are in his blood. It's no wonder he would seek outlets like jujitsu to relieve the pressure of his life. I'm not sure where I'll fit into that life. The girl from foster care with vintage t-shirts, who prefers vinyl records to digital downloads, and manages bands doesn't exactly exemplify that trophy wife image.

His arms snake around my waist and pulls my body to his chest. "What's rolling around in that head of yours?" he asks playfully as he kisses my neck. "I've found that to be a dangerous place to be."

I turn in his arms and wrap my arms around his shoulders. "What do you see when you look at me?"

"I'm not sure I want to answer that question. It feels like a trick." A serious tone laces his voice, all playfulness is absent from his delivery. I scowl, so he continues his explanation. "No matter how I answer, Campbell, I don't think it will be what you're looking for."

He's right.

My mind is attempting to force my heart into believing he and I are an impossibility. No matter how he answered, I would find a way to discredit our predicament. For all the advice I offer so freely to others, I struggle to follow it myself.

"I just need to know that you're sure," I try to explain.

He rubs his hands lightly up and down my back. Sneaking under my shirt, he traces lines and swirl patterns with his fingertips on my skin, lighting it ablaze. "I've never been more sure of anything in my life, Campbell," he whispers into my ear. "Now that I have you, I don't plan on ever letting you go. So prepare that mind of yours to stop overthinking everything."

He kisses my forehead, prompting my eyes to close, savoring the closeness. "Okay," I murmur. "I'm done fighting. If you're here, I'm here."

"I'm not going anywhere, and neither are you, love." He leans in and kisses me carefully. Instead of the passion and fire of the elevator, his stature is now the epitome of tenderness and care. He's speaking to my heart, and it is absolutely listening. I'm in so deep; I'm not sure how I could ever really backpedal from this, from him.

A knock at the door interrupts us. "You have got to be kidding me," Lakin groans. "I don't think we will ever catch a break."

I give him a chaste peck on the lips and push him toward the door to pay for our dinner. He reluctantly leaves my side and I find a spot on the couch.

When he returns holding the pizza, soda, and cake, he nods toward his bedroom. "Grab a blanket from the closet, let's go have a picnic."

I hop up and throw the large fleece blanket draped across the back of the couch around my arm and follow him to his room. I spread it out on the hardwood floor and he places all of the food items on the blanket. "Wait here, I'll go get some plates and napkins," he says as I open the lid and allow the delicious aroma of sweet marinara sauce and mozzarella cheese to fill the air. I wave him off as I grab a slice and stuff the first magical bite into my mouth.

Lakin

I move as quickly as I can, grabbing anything I think we may need for our picnic. I don't want to waste a single second with Campbell, now that I finally have her tangled in my web. If I can at all help it, I never want to let this girl go.

I pause in the doorway when I return and just enjoy the scenery. This girl I'm smitten with has already made herself at home by starting a movie and sprawling out on the blanket. She giggles with each comedic scene and I'm enthralled by the beauty before me.

A small chuckle escapes my lips and she turns to find me spying on her. "You better hurry and get over here or I can't promise how much pizza will be left for you," she says, patting the floor beside her.

I pull the cake I ordered out of the bag and place it in front of her. "I'm not worried. I'm saving space for dessert," I tell her with a smile. Her eyes widen in disbelief and she immediately sits up and crosses her legs to examine the confessionary creation.

"You got me a birthday cake?" she asks, her fingers lightly touching the plastic lid.

"I originally got you cupcakes, but those ended up on the lobby floor. This was plan B." I remove the lid and stick a candle in the center. It doesn't even have her name on it, but it's still a cake, so I figure the thought counts for at least something. "Sorry it's not much," I add.

Her eyes instantly flash to mine, holding me ransom. "It's everything," she says. Her eyes filling with tears, she smiles to distract herself from the emotion.

I lean in and light the candle before kissing her cheek. "I will give you everything, Campbell. All you have to do is wish for it," I whisper into her ear.

I pull away and scoot the cake closer to her, motioning for her to blow out the candle. She takes her time, contemplating her options before finally closing her eyes and lightly blowing out the candle. A grin hits her lips before she even opens her eyes again, and my heart swells knowing that my simple act put that smile in place.

"Happy birthday, Campbell."

"Thank you, Lakin. For everything, thank you."

I nod and dip my finger in the silky chocolate frosting. Playfully holding up my finger, I offer it to her and she hesitates before taking my finger into her mouth. The appreciative sigh escaping her mouth makes my body hyperaware. I've been holding back for so long, now that I have the go ahead, I find it excruciating to restrain myself. I want to devour her, but I know being too forward will only scare her away.

Her taste buds tickle the pad of my finger, and my mind dances thinking about what it would feel like to have that tongue wrapped around other areas. I've had women—who am I fucking kidding? I've had a lot of women—but I have never wanted any of them as much as I want Campbell. I have never wanted anything more than meaningless sex with any of them, but with Cam, I want more. I want to give more, take more. I want it all.

She finally releases my finger and I use my thumb to rub the remnants of chocolate off her bottom lip as my palm rests on her cheek. Before I can talk myself out of it once again, I lean in and replace my thumb with my lips.

She tastes divine, but I proceed lightly, delicately cradling her face in my hands as I kiss her silky lips. She pulls away with a smile and reaches up, removing the ponytail holder from her hair. Her ebony locks fall down in waves beyond her shoulders, and I lose whatever resolve I once had…but so does she.

We both rise up onto our knees and crash together in the middle of the blanket. My fingers tangle into her hair and she wraps her arms around my shoulders, pulling me to her. It's a feverish frenzy of kissing and tugging at clothing, each of us stripping the other bare. It's a year's worth of attraction, a year's worth of yearning, spilling out into the best moment I've ever experienced.

I wind my arms around her and pick her up. "Bed," I say between kisses. "I need you in my bed." She nods and wraps her legs around my waist.

"I've waited so long for you, Cam. You know I'm never letting go, right?" I murmur as I carry her to my bed, nibbling on her neck.

"Then hang on," she says coyly. Her words float in the air, spurring me on further.

I lay her across the white blankets on my bed and take a moment to appreciate her beautifully naked body. I want to burn every curve, every freckle into memory. She reaches for the blanket to cover up, uncomfortable with my stare.

"No, Cam, don't. You're gorgeous, love. I just want to see you, appreciate you."

Clearly nervous, she takes a deep breath and fixes the rumpled duvet.

I crawl up the bed and cover her body with my own; her skin against mine feels amazing. "Let me show you," I say, searching her eyes, reassuring her of my feelings.

Her hand snakes into my hair and cups the back of my neck, pulling me down to her. Her eyes never lose their hold on mine. "Show me then," she whispers.

I smash my lips to hers, my hands exploring the curves I adore.

Slowly, I sink into a bliss I've never known.

Baring my soul, I wedge myself into the heart of the only woman I've ever wanted to hold forever.

We find oblivion in something neither of us have ever had, nor wanted…until now.

Lakin

"You know, I never got to eat my birthday cake," Campbell says as she lackadaisically swirls her fingernails across my chest. Our bodies are tangled and twisted together, the blankets and sheets in complete disarray.

"That's not true. I distinctly remember you tasting the frosting. Besides, sex is always better than cake."

She rises up from my shoulder. "Blasphemy," she declares.

"Okay, how about sex with me is always better?" I chuckle and she nestles back into the crook of my shoulder.

"Oh shit, I forgot your birthday present," I exclaim, bouncing Campbell from our comfortable cocoon as I struggle to get out of the bed.

"I think you and the cake were present enough, Mr. Ryan," she jokes, wrapping a sheet around her body.

"I'll be right back," I say excitedly as I pull my boxers briefs on and dash out of the bedroom in search of her gift. I had it in my jacket pocket earlier tonight, but locating the jacket proves difficult. I let out a sigh of relief when I reach into the pocket and brush my fingers along the edges of the box. Now that I can truly call Campbell mine, this present takes on a whole new meaning. I'm so glad I took the risk to buy it.

I race back to my bedroom and playfully hop onto my bed next to Campbell. "You're ridiculous," she laughs before kissing her fingertips and touching them to my cheek.

When she attempts to pull her hand back, I grab her wrist and bring her fingers to my mouth, kissing the pads of her tiny fingers. "Close your eyes," I tell her.

She hesitantly complies and I turn her hand over, palm up. I place the small box wrapped in shiny blue paper with a black bow in her hand and scoot back on the bed.

"Okay, open your eyes," I tell her once I've given her a little space.

"Blue." She grins. "Did you wrap it yourself?" she asks.

"I know it's your favorite," I say. "I have to admit, though, I went through a whole roll trying to wrap it. I now know why I have all Christmas presents gift wrapped at the stores; wrapping is a bitch."

She giggles. "Well, I appreciate the thought. I know I haven't received a lot of gifts in my life, but I would say you nailed the wrapping job."

"I wasn't going to let someone else package this, nor any other future gifts for you, Cam. Let this be the first of many, love," I tell her, encouraging her to finally open the present.

My excitement is willing her to just tear it open, but she does no such thing. She slides her finger under the tape and lightly separates the paper, careful not to tear it. She folds the paper and lays it gently on the bed, like she would use it for some future gift.

Her eyes widen when she uncovers the square jewelry box. She immediately looks to me and fumbles to say anything coherent.

"Simmer down, Cam," I laugh. "I'm young and in love, but I'm not stupid. I get that marriage is off the table. Just open it."

She relaxes at my words and snaps open the box. Immediately she frowns, misunderstanding the pendant that lies inside.

I take it from the box and hold the gold circle in my hand. She snaps the box shut and places it next to the paper.

"This is a love token. Women used to send their soldiers to war with a token of their love around their necks. It was usually a coin that had a hole in it. It was a reminder that no matter what they faced, not to forget the comfort of the love they had at home. So, I had this one designed for us."

"Am I going somewhere?" she asks hesitantly.

"You've already been to war, Campbell. That necklace you wear now is a reminder of that. This one is different."

She protectively grips the flower necklace that hangs from her neck. I've never seen her without the necklace; I'm aware of its value to her. She's told me a foster parent, Sharon, gave it to her, and although she's shared little else about it, I understand its significance.

I show her the same flower engraved into the white gold pendant. "It's always important to remember where we come from, even if it's painful to think about," I explain, rubbing my finger across the forget-me-not on the medallion. "But this," I say turning the token over to reveal the words inscribed, "is the promise of your future."

"What does it say?" she asks, taking the token from me and examining the Irish words etched into the metal. Both of our last names are derived from Irish and English origins dating back to the Norman Conquest of 1066. So I thought it fitting that Gaelic be used on her gift to reflect the words that connect us.

"Forget me not, my love," I tell her. "These words, this token, is your past, your present, and hopefully a future with me. I've wanted to be with you since the night I met you at the bar with Brooks, and I have never been able to untangle myself from your web. I know I'm not the relationship guy. I realize I'm a risk, and I absolutely know that you're scared of what attachments could do to your heart. I'm not asking you to wear it right now; honestly, I don't want you to. When you're ready to take a more permanent leap with me, that's when I'd like to see it around your neck."

Her eyes move from mine and fixate on the token, no doubt mulling over my explanation. "I don't know what to say."

"Campbell, I–"

"No, let me get this out," she interrupts, before bowing her head, hiding her eyes from me. "I don't share with people about how I grew up; I don't want people to think that where I came from is all there is to me."

She pauses and I reach for her, grabbing her hand to thread our fingers together.

"There are things that happened that I don't know if I'll ever be able to share with you, Lakin. But I need you to know that what you did for me this evening, the cake, this gift…it's overwhelming. It reminds me of all the things I never had while at the same time, it makes me so thankful it's you here to offer me these things."

I take the token from her and place it back into its case. Her body immediately relaxes as I alleviate the pressure of the moment. "Thank you," she exhales when she hears the box snap shut.

I rest the box in her palm and then lightly lift her chin with my fingers. I need to see her eyes; she needs to see mine. They are the windows to my soul, and I want Campbell to look through to see my sincerity.

"Cam, I'm not going anywhere," I say softly. "This…me…us, it's yours when you're ready."

She smiles and leans into me, instigating a kiss. A needy, scorching kiss that only Cam could deliver. I would forever walk through fire to be on the receiving end of her attention.

I only hope she forgets me not.

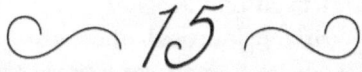

Campbell

I shoot a text to Jen and settle back into the sofa in the lounge area of the bridal shop. That girl is notoriously late; she's lucky we love her anyways.

"What did she say?" Vivian asks as she sits next to me and rummages through her giant mom bag. "I don't know how long they'll hold our appointment," she adds when she finds her lip gloss and lathers her lips in shimmer.

Standing next to a rack of fluffy bridesmaids dress, Carly pulls one off the rack and holds it up to her frame. "Why don't we just start picking things out so she has some options when she gets her?"

Olivia pulls down a dress for herself, ripping it away from the hanger. "Ohhh, pretty, Momma," she says, rubbing the silky fabric between her petite fingers.

"Liv, honey, look don't touch. Let's put it back on the hanger," Carly patiently reminds her as she takes the bridesmaid dress from Olivia's hands and places it back on the rack. I'm zoned into the interaction between the two when my phone vibrates in my hand, alerting me of a text message.

I casually look down, expecting Jen's name to flash across the screen, but instead Lakin's is there.

"Is that Jen?" Vivian asks, attempting to peer at the message. "Tell her to get her ass here pronto."

When she looks at Carly to apologize for her foul language, I try to hide my phone as nonchalantly as possible. I can feel my face flush and I take a deep breath to compose myself. I swipe the lock screen and the text brings a smile to my face.

> *Lakin: Just wanted to let you know I was thinking about you. Have a good day with the girls.*

"Well? Is she almost here?" Carly inquires.

"Um, yeah, like fifteen minutes away," I lie. She rolls her eyes and goes back to searching through the racks of dresses. Vivian then stands and catches up to the sales woman who is supposed to help us today.

I direct my attention back to my phone and hover my fingers over the keypad to send a message back to him, unsure of what to say. My phone buzzes again before I get anything typed.

> *Lakin: Dinner tonight.*

> *Me: Shouldn't you be working?*

> *Lakin: Avoidance, just like that, huh?*

> *Me: I'm proficient at only a few things, avoidance happens to be one of them.*

> *Lakin: I'd say you scored advanced in many categories last night.*

Whatever flush I had before, is now flaming red. My ears are on fire from the embarrassment his words provoke. My eyes scan the boutique, pinning the location of everyone, making sure my conversation isn't discovered.

> *Lakin: Dinner, it wasn't a question. I'll see you at 7, Cam.*

I can't help but grin. This man has turned everything upside down. He goes against everything I tried to protect myself from, but I've found him to be the hardest thing to resist. Lakin has aggressively pursued a relationship and I have aggressively avoided one. But no matter how hard I struggle out of his grasp, he's captured me and claimed my heart. My fear of him letting go of us is stronger than anything I was ever afraid of before him. I let my heart lead, and type the words it demands.

> *Me: See you then.*

> *Lakin: Nabac dom gan, mo ghrá.*

And there it is, the affirmation I needed...'forget me not, my love.' He gave me the necklace last night, but it's tucked into a pocket in my purse. I feel it beckoning me to put it on, those words calling to me, but I'm not brave enough to wear it. Not yet.

Commotion at the store entrance pulls my attention away from my thoughts of Lakin. Jen's voice reverberates through the establishment. She has no concept of the other people in the store. Today is her dress day and apparently, everyone at this bridal shop needs to be aware of that fact. It's Jen's world and we are just living in it.

"Sorry, I'm late, girls!" she shouts from across the store. Carly's eyes widen and she ducks behind the rack next to her in mortification. Vivian bows her head and shakes it, acknowledging Jen's antics will never change. An engagement, kids, none of it has mellowed our spunky spitfire.

"Jen, there is a store full of other people, and their day is getting messed up by your entrance," I say, hushing her.

She looks around and scrunches her face in understanding, but then shrugs her shoulders and moves closer to us all, pulling us each in for a hug. Yup, teachable moment is over and forgotten.

"I had to drop off the kiddos with Casen and the guys so we could just have us girls today," she says before turning to Carly and Olivia. "I thought this was an adult day?" she adds pointedly at Carly.

Carly diverts her eyes. "I didn't have childcare. I thought it would be more important that I was here with Olivia, than not at all."

"I call bullshit," Jen responds quickly. "You know Casen, Brooks, hell any one of the guys would have watched her today. I'll let it slide, chica," she says, pointing her finger at Carly. "But you better arrange a sitter for my bachelorette party. It's all planned...Vegas, baby," she says, nodding her head at each one of us, grinning widely.

"No way, not happening," Vivian interjects. "I have four children, including an infant. There is no way I can run off and leave Brooks with the kids all weekend."

"What do you mean? Brooks is coming too. It's a joint bachelor-bachelorette party!" Jen exclaims.

"Did you sustain some kind of brain injury on the way here? What in the world would make you think we can all just drop everything, including our children, and run off to Vegas?" Carly asks. "Besides, the wedding is several months away, why have it now?"

Jen looks to me for my opinion, and I know she's not going to like my answer. When I stall in my delivery, her brow scrunches in disappointment.

"Please, you guys. I feel like we are all getting so wrapped up in our individual lives. Our men, our kids…" she looks to me and adds, "our careers." She grabs my hand, her eyes pleading with me. "I just want one weekend for us, like old times. In college, we didn't have to give a shit; we had no responsibilities. We only had to worry about ourselves and each other. I want that again for just one weekend."

I search each of my friends' expressions. They are all looking to me for direction on this one. "Fine," I say, exhaling loudly. I look at both Carly and Vivian. "It's one weekend. Fly in Friday, be home by Sunday, surely we can pull that off."

"I'll have to talk to Brooks, but I'm sure between Katie and our parents keeping the kids, we can go," Vivian resigns.

Carly nervously bites her lip, unsure of what to do or how to respond to her friends. Her expression is pained. I know she doesn't want to let anyone down, but she also doesn't want Jack to think she's not being a good mother either. That's exactly what he would think of her if he found out she ran off to Vegas for the weekend, bachelorette party or not.

Vivian must sense the same uncertainty I am, because she quickly offers an out for her mental indecision. "If Jack isn't around to keep her, Olivia can always stay with our kiddos. No one will mind a bit."

Carly's body relaxes and her frown softens into an easy smile. "Thank you for that, Viv. If it isn't a bother, I would rather her go with you guys than Jack. I really don't even want him aware of the trip. He'll only make a big deal out of it."

Vivian tilts her head, reading between the lines. "How's everything going with Jack? Is he making everything more difficult?"

I look around for Olivia to make sure she's outside of earshot. She doesn't need to hear the verbal bashing that her father is about to receive. Carly, I can see, is thinking the same thing because she doesn't speak until she confirms Olivia is too far away and too engrossed in the dresses she's looking at to hear the conversation.

"You know at first, he tried to make me feel stupid, like it was nothing and I just misunderstood an innocent friendship. He insisted the vasectomy was his way of taking the pressure off of me to have more children, so we could look into other options like adoption. He wanted us to go to counseling and work things out," she explains.

"Bullshit. There is no mistaking what we saw on that video," Jen insists.

She is absolutely correct. The video I gave Carly was edited. There was plenty more to show if necessary, but I felt that was enough to give her the push in the right direction. I didn't need to shove the affair in her face; she saw what she needed to.

"I agree. He's just trying to take advantage of my emotions, and if he really thought he could talk his way out of any wrong-doing, then he must have never had too much respect for me, or my intelligence, in the first place."

"Fuck him," Jen spouts off. Vivian immediately glares at her and then searches the store for any eavesdropping ears. When Carly shows offense for her use of language, Jen relents and apologizes.

"Yeah, well, once he realized I wasn't going to take him back, he's gotten rather nasty about things. He criticizes me any chance he gets. He tries to guilt me into thinking the divorce is my fault because we had a less than stellar sex life. That I'm homely and I'll never find any other man, so I might as well come back because he's the only one who would be all right with the way I look."

Her shoulders sag, and it's evident this man has completely torn down every bit of her self-confidence. I maintain a cool demeanor; however, I want to hunt this man down and make him pay for ever hurting my friend this way. After I'm done with him, he'll regret ever treating a woman this way.

"I'm going to kill him," Vivian steams, her rage rolling off her. She is typically the most sensitive, caring woman, but if her fiery temper flares, Hell hath no fury.

"It's fine. I get that I'm not much to look at right now. I've been in mommy mode and let my appearance go," Carly tries to explain her mom jeans, lack of make-up, and pony tail, but I think there is more to it than that. She's always been the self-conscious one in the group. She's curvy in a way that men usually love, but the average female hates. While she hides her figure because she's insecure, men drool over her cleavage and bubble butt. She has no idea how truly beautiful she is, and it sounds like Jack helped to trap her in that box of self-doubt.

"Well, girly, we are going to fix this situation, ASAP," Vivian declares wrapping her arm around Carly's shoulder and giving her a light squeeze.

"What do you mean?" she asks, bracing for the devious plan Vivian and Jen are obviously hatching.

"We love you, chica, and you've got a lot to work with." Jen waves her hands around Carly's body, highlighting her assets. "But I'm thinking at little less Ally Sheedy from the Breakfast Club and a little more hot momma from the burbs." Jen circles her hands around Carly's mess of a hairstyle. I cover my mouth to hide the small laugh that escapes my lips. Jen has absolutely no filter, but in this case, it's our job as friends to help Carly make the transition into single life again. How the girls at her spa haven't gotten a hold of her, I'll never know, but the girl needs to be dolled up a bit.

"You know, Jen, just because you add an 'I love you' at the beginning, it doesn't make your comment any less insulting," Carly huffs and plops herself next to me on the couch.

"Sorry. It's just that, well…" She stalls, collecting her thoughts. "I always say the best way to get over a man is to get under another one. I'm your friend and you need me to help get your mojo back, whether you think so or not." Jen looks to Vivian, who is one step ahead and is on her phone booking an appointment with her salon for Carly. "We are going to have you so smokin' that you will be the object of every man's affection in Vegas. You will have your pick!" Jen lightly claps her hands and bounces on her toes in excitement.

"The last thing I need is another man," Carly declares. "I just want to feel better about myself, and I don't need a man to do that."

"Maybe not, but you do need a little hair product," Jen laughs, attempting to pat her hair down. "Girl, you are one hot mess right now."

Carly swats Jen's hand away and looks to me seeking I don't know what…approval, maybe a safety line, neither of which I'll give her. Instead I offer a smile and the only words that make sense. "It's time to find our Carly again."

She understands and smiles back, a smile we haven't seen from her in years. "Okay," she murmurs.

Vivian tapped on her smartphone and throws it into her purse. "All done," she announces. "You have an appointment at my salon. We will have you all fixed up and feeling good in no time."

Lakin

I don't know what I did in a past life to deserve the life I have now, but I'm guessing I was some awesome kind of dude. Success in school and business have always came easy for me, and in the women department, well, I never had any issues. However, I had never upgraded any of those exchanges to relationship status. They were exacting that…exchanges. Somehow, though I have found myself in a relationship I never thought I wanted until I met her, and I couldn't be fucking happier to be tied to her. Campbell is everything I never knew I wanted.

Tonight is going to be a first for both of us.

I told her to wear a pair of her most comfortable jeans and a t-shirt. I refused to tell her where we were going so she was a little apprehensive. As I pulled up to her apartment to pick her up, though, she bounded down the stairs in the attire I requested with a bright smile ready for whatever I planned to throw at her.

"I was going to come up and get you," I say as I open the passenger side door for her. Shit, I'm trying to be Prince Charming here, and she stole my thunder. This is a date after all.

"Sorry," she says sheepishly. "I'm just so excited. You have been very elusive about what we are doing tonight." She kisses me on the cheek and settles into her seat. I pause momentarily, letting her affection absorb into my skin, savoring every second of the feeling.

I rub my hand across the skin that her lips touched, before making my way back around the car, and sliding into the driver's seat. I look at her once again before throwing the car in drive and speeding out of her building complex.

I smile to myself as she stares out of the window.

She's right. I have given her absolutely no clues about tonight and I offer nothing more on the way to our final destination. The traffic is heavy and as we approach the swarms of people crowding the downtown streets, I assume she has figured out where we are going. However, as we pull into the stadium, I realize this really is a night of firsts.

"Wow, is there an outdoor festival or concert or something going on?" she asks. "The streets are packed."

"No," I chuckle. "There is a Rockies game tonight."

"Oh, I don't really follow basketball," she shrugs.

My head whips around to looks at her. Did she really just say that the Colorado Rockies were a basketball team? I shake my head and laugh.

"Baseball," I simply say.

"Same difference," she says nonchalantly. "They are both played with balls."

I now remember why I've never taken a woman to a ballgame. Unless they can truly appreciate the game, the most fun they have is during the seventh inning stretch when the crowd sings "Take Me Out to the Ballgame." I'm hoping that this brilliant attempt at a fun date, doesn't completely crash and burn.

I find decent parking near Coors Field and we briskly follow the crowd. I thread my fingers with hers and lead her along the sidewalks, weaving around the people lingering on the path. It feels good to have her tucked into my side. If I have my way, it's a place she'll never leave.

It isn't until I'm handing our tickets to the gate attendant that she puts it together.

"Do they have other events here or are we actually going to the game?" she asks, not exactly thrilled at her prospects for the evening. "You know I know nothing about sports, right?"

My smile widens. Tonight is going to be so much fun. This is her first baseball game and will be a night neither of us will forget. I don't answer her, instead, I pull her toward our seats before she can change her mind about our evening.

I usually watch the game from my company's box seats, but tonight, with Campbell in tow, I bought tickets along the third baseline. I want her to experience the game as a true fan would. Mingling with the crowd, the smell of the beer and hotdogs, taking part in the wave, she needs to be immersed in the action.

We find our seats and I immediately flag the guy selling beers.

"I know you're not much of a drinker but baseball games and a cold one kind of go hand in hand," I explain as I hand her the plastic bottle of beer. She nods and offers a tight smile, before taking a small, sampling of the ale. I know that is probably the most that she'll drink of it, but it is still worth the eight bucks even if she just holds it all night.

Her unease at the situation is evident. Campbell likes having the upper hand. She like being prepared for any situation. Baseball is not her cup of tea, and there is no way that she can fake it.

"We are here to have fun together, Cam. I could give two shits whether you know anything about baseball. We are here for the experience of the surroundings, and to enjoy each other's company, that's all."

I place my hand on her knee and gently give it a squeeze until I see her relax and smile. Apparently, that's all that needs to be said. By the second inning, she is shouting at the umpires, referring to them as zebras…yeah, wrong sport. She is high-fiving all the fans in the general vicinity any time one of "our guys" as she refers to them does something "cool looking." Any other woman, and I probably would have excused myself to the bathroom and hightailed it out of the stadium, but Campbell has made this night something to remember. Here I thought I would create something special for her, and all the while, she has done that for me.

"Travelling!" she shouts when the player on first attempts to steal second.

"That's basketball," I laugh. "It's called stealing, not travelling,"

"Well damn, we may need to go to a basketball game next, because I sure know a lot of basketball lingo. I'm like the sports whisperer." She laughs and the sound is so contagious, that I can't help but join in.

I wrap my arm around her waist, pulling her to me until I can nuzzle into her neck. "I'll take you anywhere you want to, Cam," I murmur against her delicate skin. "As long as you know you can't get rid of me."

The crack of the bat connecting with the ball sends the crowd around us to their feet. A roar of cheers makes it impossible to hear her, but her actions speak louder than anyone around us.

Pulling away from me, she momentarily searches my eyes. Grabbing my t-shirt and twisting the collar in her grip she smashes my body to hers. "I'm not going anywhere," she says against my lips before she takes complete control and crashes her lips to mine.

If I ever had any doubt that Campbell would follow through on this new journey we have set course on, it evaporated in that moment.

She was mine, and for the first time ever, a woman has been able to say with certainty that I was completely hers.

Campbell

In light of everything that has gone on, Jen's idea about taking a mini Vegas vacation doesn't seem so bad, even if it's a bachelorette party. Everyone has been preparing for the weekend that is supposed to surpass all weekends. I've stayed grounded though, wrapped in the reality of the present.

Since Sharon died, Evan has called or texted nearly twice a week, making sure I'm okay. I think more than anything, he just wants to hear a friendly voice that cared for his mom as much as he did. It took a while, but I've finally come to terms with her passing. I've spent a large amount of time either with Lakin or at the foundation. I'm hopeful each time I've been back that I will run into Leah again, but I have yet to see her.

While Lakin gave me the file on Leah the day Sharon died, I haven't been able to bring myself to look through it. I guess I'm hoping she will tell me her story herself. That, or I fear what I might find will open old wounds. Those wounds have long ago scabbed over, but I'm still waiting for the scars to fade.

I don't dig into my past often, but somehow this girl with just one meeting has brought it all back.

When I first arrive at the foundation, I walk down the hallway through the administration portion of the building. Vivian's office door is open, but she isn't in it. I step inside, take Leah's file out of my backpack, and lightly lay it across Vivian's desk. It's thick, the manila folder barely able to hold the papers within it. Without even looking inside, I know she either has been in the system a long time or has had several placements.

I slowly roll the chair from the desk and slide my body into the seat. I inhale deeply and release every bit of air in my lungs before I flip open the front cover of the folder. If anyone was walking by at that moment, they probably would have heard the sound of my heart cracking into shattered pieces and would have seen all resemblance of bravery spilling out onto the paper.

I attempt to read the first page, but as my eyes scan it, the words blur with tears. The red ink in large print at the bottom, reads loud and clear though:

PARENTAL RIGHTS TERMINATED.
AVAILABLE FOR ADOPTION.

In the six years she has been in the system, it looks as though Leah has had multiple placements. She bounced from foster home, back to her mother, and then back to foster homes over and over again until last year when her mother's rights were finally terminated by the court and she was placed in a group facility.

There are no reports of sexual abuse or even physical abuse. She was removed from her mother's care because of neglect. Documentation outlining a life with drugs in the home, her being left alone for days, weeks at a time, even a lack of food in the house filled the file. There lacks detailed explanations for the multiple placements, nor are there details as to why reunification with her mother did not work after so many years in the system. Those specifics will have to come from the caseworker or Leah herself.

After reading what is available, though, I want, more than ever, to find this girl and help her, if I can. There have been moments when I thought, I could be this girl's mother; I could take that on. Reality sinks in though, and I know that just isn't possible. My job has me constantly on the road in and out of bars half of the year, touring with bands. This girl needs a family, a real mom that is present. She needs someone who can help with homework and teenage drama, and that's just not me.

I close the file and stuff it back into my backpack. I envision letting her shred it or maybe burning it one day, just like I wish I could have with my own file. I know these are just pieced together copies of the original file, but it still would mean something to see it buried.

Standing, I sling my bag over my shoulder and make my way down the hall toward the commons room where I first met her. Every time I've been back, I look to the couch, hoping to see her there reading poetry, but over and over again I've been disappointed.

The room is crowded with kids, and the smell of sweaty teenagers from the summer heat hits me. Denver has a mixture of schools, which vary from year-round to traditional schedules, so even though it's the middle of the summer, some of them will be working on assignments for school, while for others, the school year is a distant memory.

I walk directly to the sign-in sheet at the front desk. My finger scrolls down the list of names and I'm met with disappointment when I reach the end of the list without coming across Leah's name. I exhale my frustration and turn to the kids in the room to see where I'll be most helpful for the afternoon.

Then I see the flowing locks of blonde hair that I have been so eager to see again. Sitting in the same spot as before, Leah is stretched out on the couch, hoisting up a mammoth of a book: *The Complete Tales and Poems of Edgar Allan Poe.* Her brows are drawn together, deep in thought, and I smile to myself at the scene before me.

"It's been I while," I say as I approach her. "I hoped I would find you here, and with a book on Poe is an even better surprise."

She looks up at me with tears in her eyes, which she hurriedly wipes away. She doesn't want me to see her weakness, but it's too late. It was there; I saw it.

"It took a while before I could get to the library, and I wanted to have this book before I came here again. You know, in case you were here," she explains. She clears her throat to rid herself of the emotion that overtook her, but I can still hear the slight tremble in her voice.

I take my seat next to her and change the subject as not to bring attention to her obvious discomfort and my intrusion of her personal moment.

"I'm glad to see you here again. I have to admit, I was happy to see that book in your hands. Are you enjoying it?"

She runs her hand across the pages she was just reading, and lets out a sigh. "Yes," she says looking down at the book. "It's like the words are speaking to me, and well, some hit a little too close to home."

I peer over to look at the page and read the passage that she has lightly starred with a pencil.

"The boundaries which divide Life from Death are at best shadowy and vague. Who shall say where the one ends, and where the other begins?" I read aloud and nod.

Leah takes a ragged breath and searches my eyes. She's looking for a safe place, a safe person, to share her secrets, and I try to convey that I understand her struggle. I, too, have felt the pain of this world.

She begins to speak, but the words lodge in her throat and she stammers for a moment. "After my father left us, my mom just gave up. There were times she tried, but her pain was too great. She used to say the drugs helped her forget her loss, helped her not feel. No matter how many times I was taken away, I tried to do things to find my way back to her. I didn't want anyone to want me so I could be with my mom."

A tear escapes her eye and slides down her cheek, and this time she's slow to wipe it away.

"I ran away more times than I can count. I really thought I could take care of her, but I could never fix her. There were times when she would take off and I found myself alone...scared....hungry. I wasn't sure if she was alive or dead. There were times, I didn't care; I just wanted it to be over."

I move closer to her on the couch and reach my hands out for her to give me the book. She hands it over willingly and I turn the pages to the poem I want to share with her.

"There was a time when I had no place to go," I tell her. "No one to run to."

She tilts her head, confused by my admission.

"My parents died when I was little and there was no one," I clarify. "I was alone. Then, just before I graduated high school, I met a family that made a home for me. I was never adopted, but I found a home nonetheless. Now, I have managed to create a family for myself, with those I surround myself with. I guess you could say I was blessed to get to choose my family."

I hand her back the book with the page of the poem open for her to read. I point to a line and she reads aloud. "Never to suffer would never to have been blessed," she whispers.

Her eyes don't move from the page; she lets the words settle on her, sink into the fabric of her identity. "I figure if I hadn't experienced the pain of my past, I would never have been able to appreciate the gifts I have in my present," I murmur. "Do you think you're ready now to accept what the world could offer for you?"

She doesn't hesitate; her head snaps up and her eyes meet mine. "Absolutely," she says confidently. "I know I've missed my chance for a family, but someday I would like to create my own, just like you did."

"It's never too late, Leah. You just haven't met the right people yet. I promise to help change that." I know I'm breaking a huge rule here; I should never promise something I may not be able to follow through on. I need to make her believe she hasn't experienced the hell she has for nothing, though, that there are great things in store for her and she will be loved…like all kids should be.

I pull out my phone and scroll through the numbers until I come across the number I'm looking for. A person with the biggest heart I know, someone who would care for this child like her own, and who deserves a happily ever after just as much as the girl sitting next to me.

Leah scowls, the line between her brows creating a deep divide. "I'm starting right now," I tell her with a smile and stand from the couch. I raise my finger to Leah to stay put as I walk away from the couch. The phone rings and I hold my breath, waiting for her to finally pick up.

"Hey, Cam. What's up," she says cheerfully through the phone.

A rush of air leaves my body as I try to steady my voice. I don't usually ask for much from these girls, but in this instance, I'll be asking for everything.

"Can we meet?" I ask. "There is something important I want to talk to you about."

"Sure," she says. "The plane for Vegas leaves in the morning; how about we meet just before?"

"Thank you. See you in the morning, Carly."

Carly

I could have guessed a million and a half reasons why Campbell wanted to talk to me, and I would have never been correct. As much as I wanted to have more children, the thought of fostering a teenager, one I've never even met, no less, is something I never would have thought to consider.

My divorce isn't final yet, I'm just getting on my feet, and I don't think I would even be approved to be a foster parent as a single person. Campbell was quick to squash all negativity and misinformation I had about the process, but still, I need time to think about the possibility of bringing someone into my home…into my life.

While Campbell thought the decision was a no brainer, I'm hesitant. I don't even know if I'm a strong enough person to handle the emotional back and forth that a foster parent could possibly go through.

I haven't thought of anything else since she spoke with me.

As soon as the plane landed and we caught the shuttle to our hotel, I immediately checked in and changed into my pool attire. My body went through the motions, but my brain was stuck in first gear, my thoughts with a young lady back home with no one and how her last effort for a family lies with me. I should turn Jen loose on Campbell for putting me in such a difficult situation.

My mind wrestles with the possibilities until screeching from the other side of the hotel lobby puts an immediate halt to my wondering thoughts.

"Woohoo, hot momma!" Jen shouts from across the room, drawing the attention of everyone in the near vicinity. My eyes widen and I search the area for people who have honed in their attention on the obnoxious interruption. Completely mortified, I cover my face from onlookers and l scurry over to my friends as quickly as my legs can carry me. We agreed to meet in the lobby before going to the pool, and I'm now regretting that decision.

"Seriously, Jen, we are in public. You could exercise just a little restraint," I say when I finally reach her.

She bounces up and down on her toes, excitement from the Vegas atmosphere written all over her face. "Oh, simmer down, girly," she says, wrapping her arm through mine. "Look around. We will probably never see any of these people ever again. Don't worry about what they think. We are here to let our hair down and have fun. So, get with it!"

With each sentence, her voice grows in volume until her pep talk feels more like a motivational speech for an audience of a thousand. I look back to both Campbell and Vivian, who are following behind us, grinning at the ridiculousness of Jen's very public announcements and my embarrassment. I roll my eyes at them and allow her to drag me toward the pool entrance.

Jen smiles and giggles as she continues to speak about all of the fun we will have and all the men she will throw my way as a christening back to singlehood.

The sun nearly blinds me when we step outside, and I slide my sunglasses down off my head to block the light. Tanned bodies of twenty-somethings line the poolside and have taken over the first rows of lawn chairs.

Snaking through the chairs, Jen leads us toward a roped off cabana area that shows a "Reserved" sign hanging from the tent. Chairs, inside and outside the tent, as well as coolers and tables fill the space, but before we have a chance to enter, Jen suddenly stops, causing Vivian and Campbell to smash into us.

"Oh, sweet baby Jesus, what are you doing here?" Jen asks a man sunbathing outside the tent. She is absolutely not pleased with his presence and her displeasure is evident in her tone. "Casen may have invited you, but you are not invading my girls' day."

He doesn't acknowledge her tirade, instead takes a sip from his fruity umbrella drink. I have a hard time looking at his face; my eyes are too narrowed in on his tanned muscles, which are covered in tattoos. His long mess of a hairstyle is piled into a man bun on top of his head, and for the life of me, I can't figure out why Jen would be so angry at such a beautiful man.

"Royce, this is kind of a special day. Isn't there another place at the pool you could be, or go hang out with the guys?" Campbell offers.

He sets his drink on the table next to him and stretches out in the lounge chair. "I don't see the problem. I'm just catching a few rays with my girl here," he says innocently. I look to the chair next to him, and how it escaped my attention before can only be attributed to his gorgeous appearance, because he is pointing to a blow up doll lying beside him. The plastic doll is dressed in a string bikini and is wearing a blonde wig. I laugh at the pure silliness of it, but I immediately stifle it when Jen shoots me a glare that could freeze every pool within a ten mile radius.

"Are you fucking with me?" Jen spouts off. "You brought that thing?"

"Sally was a gift, remember? It was only fitting that she come with me and ward off all the unwanted girl attention I might have to dodge." He defends himself in a serious tone, but I can see the humor in his eyes.

I push my sunglasses onto my head to get a better look. This is a guy who enjoys having fun, even if it's at his own expense. I've heard Jen talk about Royce before, and I remember briefly seeing him at a few of their concerts with the girls, but I couldn't place him out of that context. Jen never had anything nice to say about Royce, and Campbell never stuck up for him, so he became forgettable to me.

Seeing him laid out before me, Royce represents a whole new level of enticement, and there is nothing about him I will forget this time. He notices my wondering eyes and shoots me a mischievous smile. My eyes evade his as quickly as I can. I feel like a high school kid who just got caught staring at her crush from across homeroom. Royce catching me is no less embarrassing than those torturous teenage moments.

Jen's eyes follow his line of sight in my direction and I may have felt the world erupt around us. She spins around and grabs his Sally doll. He hops up to save her before Jen throws her into the pool. "You seriously have to leave. Stay away, Royce…from all of us." She enunciates the end of her sentence, hinting that whatever that smile meant, he can just forget about it.

Her friends are off limits.

He follows Jen to the edge of the pool to retrieve his doll. All humor and fun has evaporated and anger is now rolling off of him.

"I'll fuck who I want, princess," he clips at her. "This town is full of easy pussy; I don't need to go fishing in a small pond for someone who will follow me home. The beauty of Vegas is that it's an ocean full of fish I'll never have to see again."

"You're gross, you know that, right?" Jen answers back.

He tucks the Sally doll under his arm and bows to us, before offering me another beaming smile. "I'm sorry to have interrupted your gorgeous day, ladies," he says politely. He then turns back to Jen and frowns. "And by the way, you're just jealous I would never offer you this flesh rocket for your hot pocket."

He turns on his heel and leaves our little group. Jen is left speechless-- for once. The three of us, however, can no longer hold it in. Together we burst into laughter, which only garners death glares from Jen.

"You guys suck," she pouts as she passes by us to get to the tent. Her childish response only makes us laugh harder.

"He had a flippin' blow up doll," Vivian chuckles as she wipes the tears from her eyes.

"I can't even explain why Jen hates him so much. I just let it go, but man that guy is funny," Campbell adds.

"And pretty hot," I add, pretending to fan myself.

"You guys still suck," Jen shouts from inside the tent.

"Oh, simmer down," I say, throwing her own words back at her. "We are here to have a good time."

We walk toward the cabana and are met by a waitress ready to bring us whatever frilly drink we need, and from the look on Jen's face, we may need several. Their service is included in the price of the cabana, and we will absolutely put this poor girl to work today.

Vivian orders margaritas for the group as we unpack our pool bags and head back out of the cabana. Throwing our towels across lounge chairs, we each take a place in the sun. We relax into the warmth of the rays, and let the sun pound down on our bodies. Well, except Vivian who puts a fashionable straw hat on her head and smothers herself in sunblock. She always says her red hair attracts the sun and she doesn't need any more freckles than she already has.

A comfortable silence settles amongst us, and we enjoy the quietness of the moment. Jen was right; kids, jobs, divorces, all the stresses from back home fade away with each tranquil breath. Our server brings us our drinks and the refreshing coolness of the sweet and sour tang are a welcome relief from the heat.

"So, I think Royce is hilarious. Why do you hate him so bad?" Campbell asks. "Aaaannd Carly practically drooled all over him and his doll, so you better have a good reason to hold up her much needed cougar prowl."

I choke and spit alcohol out all over myself and my towel. "I did no such thing," I say through coughing fits.

"There will be no naked time happening on this trip with that man. Royce is an irresponsible asshole, who cares only about himself and what he can get from someone. You just stay far away, Carly. We will find you a scrumptious man, just not that one."

I wiggle in my chair, uncomfortable with the topic of conversation. I feel like I'm on display and everyone is trying to fix me, the poor divorced woman, up. The last thing I need is a man to complicate my life even more. A one-night stand is nowhere near my radar. I never had one before I was married and there is no reason why I should start now that I'm newly single.

"There's no need to worry about me. I'm good with actual alone time," I explain. "I'm in no need of a male attention."

"Bullshit," Vivian says. "Even the best LELO in the world isn't going to replace some good old fashion lovin'."

Jen giggles. "There's no need to leave the LELO out of the mix just because a friend arrives. Broaden those horizons, ladies."

We all laugh and ease back down into our chairs. "I appreciate the thought, but I think I'll pass either way," I tell them all. "There is just too much going in my life to complicate it even more with a man." I look to Campbell, hoping she gets the hint as well, but she diverts her eyes away from me and changes the subject.

"What is the plan for tonight anyways?" Campbell asks. "I know tomorrow is the actual bachelorette party, so what is in store for this evening?"

Jen and Vivian both look to each other, and when Vivian cringes, I know our foursome is going to shrink by two. "It's so rare that we have our husbands alone, we thought that tonight we could have a date night," Vivian attempts to explain as compassionately as possible; you know, you're getting ditched and this is why.

"It's not like it's a complete waste. I thought you girls could go to a show or something," Jen chimes in.

I'm not exactly thrilled with being brought to Vegas to then be dropped like a hot potato, but I do understand. Jack and I never got to have time for just the two of us once Olivia came along. Maybe that's where the problem lied with us, not devoting enough time together for our relationship. We co-existed, but we didn't really exist together as a team.

How can I fault my friends for doing something I should have also taken time to do?

I look to Campbell, who looks equally thrilled, so I take the lead on smoothing the awkward moment out.

"There are some shows I would love to see. We'll have tons of fun, Campbell."

She smiles and steals Vivian's hat. "When you guys hear how cool our night ends up, you're going to wish you hadn't ditched us."

"Nothing you can say will tempt me away from a night alone with my fiancé," Jen says with all seriousness. "That man will be wearing my ass as a hat tonight," she adds, tapping Viv's floppy hat on Campbell's head.

Everyone takes their turn displaying grossed out expressions, snorting with laughter.

"Oh, good grief," Vivian chuckles with a sigh after catching her breath. "I was just hoping for a quiet dinner."

"I say we meet for breakfast tomorrow and fill each other in on our wild night. Deal?" Campbell suggests.

"Deal," we say in unison, clinking the glass of our drinks together.

Carly

Well, that's just great. First, I was ditched by Vivian and Jen, and now I've been stood up by Campbell. I had spent an hour picking out a cute dress and heels, then doing my hair and makeup for this evening. If I was going to have a night on the town, I figured I should look the part.

But now, the longer I sit here, the more worried I am that my effort screams working girl. I shift in my dress to cover more of my legs and adjust the straps that crisscross at my shoulders. The bartender notices my discomfort and makes his way to my end of the bar once again.

"You need anything else, doll?" he asks with a light smile.

I've been waiting at the hotel bar alone for thirty minutes and every time the bartender asks if I'm doing all right, I feel his judgement and sympathy.

My phone dings, and I momentarily ignore the bartender to read the message. I can feel my brows pull together when I read the message.

> Campbell: I'm so sorry. Something important came up. Raincheck?

If it's important, I don't want her to feel bad about leaving me behind, so instead of the single response of "K" that I want to send her, I take the high road.

> Me: No worries. I'll catch up with you in the morning.

I exhale loudly and slam my phone back down on the bar top. I don't notice the bartender still standing there until his voice cuts through my mist of disappointment.

"That bad, huh?" he says.

"Any day that my pants haven't caught on fire from my legs rubbing together, is a good flipping day," I spout out.

The middle-aged bartender looks at me like he's been painted into a corner and may have to chew off an arm or something to save himself. His discomfort is clearly evident, and in his head he's quietly wishing he hadn't asked, screw the tip.

"I'm sorry," I resign. "I'll take a shot of whatever you have that will not make me feel like such a loser," I tell him, stuffing my phone into my small purse.

Without another word, he pulls some liquor out from behind the bar and lines up a shot glass on the wood along with a few wedges of lime.

"Tequila is always good for short-term memory loss," he says, pouring the golden liquid into the glass.

"I'll take it."

"Me too," a smooth voice announces behind me. I look back to see Royce pulling out the chair beside me. "If the night has gone to such shit that the tequila shots have been brought out, I might as well join the party."

Initially, I'm speechless at his intrusion. I'm not sure whether I want him to leave because, well, his presence will only find me in trouble, but on the other hand, do I really want to sit here and wallow with a bottle of liquor alone?

I look him up and down, taking in his gorgeous physique and intoxicating cologne. How could I say no?

Jen would have a fit…but she's not here. None of my friends are here. They have all run off and left me to my own devices, and if I want to hang out with this attractive man who throws caution to the wind and enjoys life, so be it.

That's what I need tonight…fun. And Royce offers just that.

"You know what?" I say, scooting over to make room for him. "You and I are going to have a blast tonight."

The bartender pours another drink for Royce and he slams it back without using the lime as a chaser.

"It's going to be a fantastic night." He grins, smashing the glass back to the bar.

Lakin

"I can't even tag along?" I shout from across the suite. "You bring me to Vegas, make me get my own room, and now I have to roam the strip alone?"

Am I whining? Probably just a tad, but I can't help but want to spend the extra time with Campbell. As much as I understand her need to spend it all with the girls, I still want to be selfish with her.

I stretch out across the massive bed and wait for Campbell's response. She steps through the entryway from the living room portion of the hotel room and pretends to pout, mocking me.

"I think you'll manage. Besides, tomorrow night you'll be doing plenty of guy things without me," she says, curling up next to me on the mattress. I'm tempted to pin her down and smother her with attention until she forgets about Carly and refuses to leave the room.

I pull her close to me, melding her body to mine. "What can I do to make you stay?" I whisper in her ear before planting a soft kiss on her neck. A giggle erupts from her sweet mouth when my scruff from the day tickles her skin.

She finally lets out a long exhale. "I have to get in the shower so I can meet Carly. How about you meet us for drinks after the show? That piano bar in the New York New York casino is a good time; how about there?

I roll onto my back and growl at her. Drinks are not what I had in mind, but I'm a desperate man willing to take what I can get. If serving as the third wheel in a girls' night is all I can get, well, I'll go with the flow.

She plops her phone on my chest and offers her mouth for a kiss. Her lips meet mine and I have to restrain myself from deepening it and allowing the passion to overtake us.

"I'm going to jump in the shower," she says between pecks. "Carly is supposed to be texting me where to meet her. When you hear from her, please text her back to let her know I'll be there."

She lands one final kiss and hops off the bed. Painfully, I watch her strut away from me and into the bathroom. I'm a little perturbed I wasn't invited into the shower, and for a second, I consider surprising her by jumping in without an invitation. When her phone buzzes to life, I let the idea fade.

Evan: I hope you have a good time. See you when you get back. Love you.

As I read the words, an entire gamut of emotions flood my system...anger, sadness, even betrayal. I love this woman with every fiber of my being, and yet while I want to make her my wife, she's exploring other options. We never said this was an exclusive relationship, but I figured it went without saying.

Pacing the floor in front of the bed, I feel as though I could wear a hole in the carpet with each step. I don't know what to do, what to say. I've never been in a position of losing the one thing I needed the most. Fuck, maybe I never really had her in the first place.

I swipe the phone off the bed, my grip dangerously close to crushing the screen as I continue to walk. I want more than anything to be relieved of my frustration by throwing it against the wall. Instead, a somber pain takes hold and I collapse back onto the bed, my head down and shoulders hunched...defeated.

The sound of the water turning off doesn't rouse my body. I'm motionless, waiting for the execution of what's left of my heart. A few excruciating minutes pass before Campbell returns. She stops suddenly when she notices me on the bed.

"What's wrong?" she asks as she wiggles her body between my knees. I don't wrap my hands around her like I want to. I can't even look up at her for fear of what I might see—unrequited love.

I place the phone in her hand, still opened to the text she just received from Evan. "Please tell me I'm the only one," I murmur, my voice stumbling over the words, barely able to push them out.

I finally look at her, her hair a wet mess of ebony flowing down her back, face fresh and beautiful, and wearing a dress that any other day, any other moment, I would have hiked around her waist.

She frowns as she reads the message, an expression that twists my heart until it feels wrung out and lifeless. Is that a look of a woman who has been caught? Is she upset I know now she hasn't been faithful to our relationship?

"Oh, Lakin," she whispers, lightly placing her soft palm on my cheek. "There could only ever be you."

"But–" I begin to say when she covers my lips with her finger to hush me.

I search her eyes, looking for clues to my fate, and I'm met with compassion. I'm met with the same love she would see in my eyes.

"Evan is my foster brother. It's true that he loves me, no less than I love him, but not in the way you're thinking, Lakin. That man was once a boy who saved me. Rescued me from a fate that nightmares are made of."

I scoot back onto the bed and pick her up so her legs are straddling my waist. I've never forced her to tell me about her past, but in this moment, my need to know is stronger than my compassion to let it lie.

"Please tell me," I say lightly, placing my hand on her chest. "I need to know this heart. I need to know why it beats the way it does. I want to be able to grip on to it and cradle it in my hand for all eternity, but I need to know that it's mine to hold."

She closes her eyes and leans in to rest her forehead on mine. I feel each of her breaths tap against my lips, ragged, uncertain. If I could reach into her mind and soothe the uncertainty, I would give every bit of wealth, every bit of my own courage to ease her anxiety. The only thing I can do is hold her, let my body plead with her soul to share herself with me.

Finally, finally she speaks, and I'm able to exhale my own apprehension.

"It was a long time ago and there are days I wish I could forget, but there are some things that happen to us that our mind will never let us escape from," she says, her eyes still closed.

She slowly pulls away from me and searches my eyes. I plead with them, with her, to feel the safety in my arms.

She takes a deep breath and runs her nails through the hair at the base of my neck. "Evan is Sharon's son. When they took me in, he and I went to the same high school; he was a year older than I was. I was only a freshman and I was new, but he helped me adjust to everyone at school. We became friends."

She hesitates, so I brush her damp hair away from her face and softly kiss her cheek to encourage her to continue. Her legs are still tangled around me, but when she gives me a nod, I scoot back slightly to provide her the space she needs.

"I only stayed with them for a few months at first. There was an emergency case on Christmas Eve and I had to be moved so they could take in a group of siblings. Sharon and my caseworker arranged for me be able to remain at the same school for the school year, and it was fine for the first month or so. Well, fine enough. My new foster parents didn't really have much to do with me. They weren't mean to me, but they didn't care much either. I was a means to help pay their rent in the trailer park." She pauses again, gathering the strength for the next piece of information. I can feel the pain she's wrestling with, the shame that lies beneath.

"But then her brother was released from jail and he came to stay with us," she whispers. "Then everything changed."

"What did he do?" is all I can say.

"Nothing at first. He gave me the creeps so I avoided him. But then her mother got sick and she left me in her husband's care so she could be with her. They never told my caseworker, because I would have been removed."

She looks away from me and stares at the ceiling as she continues to speak. Tears roll down her face but her voice never breaks, and I'm in awe of the strength I never realized she had.

"That's when it got bad," she says. "Drugs flowed in and out of the house, and they took turns using me any way they wanted. When I tried to run, they caught me and chained me up in a back bedroom of the trailer. There were days I didn't know if I was alive or dead, and I wanted it to be over so badly that I didn't care if it was the end."

I grip onto her shirt, imagining every vile thing these two men could have done. The heat of my anger boils at the thoughts that run through my head.

"How did no one know this was going on? You just get dumped off and no one checks on you?"

She squares her shoulders to look at me. "Evan came looking," is all she says.

"What happened? Did he call the police? Contact social services? Please tell me the day he found you is the day you left that house?" My mouth can barely keep up with what I'm thinking. I rattle off questions without waiting for responses. Instead of getting shaken or upset, she continues to run her fingers through my hair to settle my emotions instead of me helping her.

"He took care of it, of me," she declares, avoiding further details.

"How? How did you get away?" I ask.

She leans in close to me as if she is going to share a secret no one knows. She grabs the back of my neck and delivers a sentence that rocks my very core.

"He killed them," she whispers.

My eyes widen.

I admit I would have done the same had I been confronted with the opportunity, but for a teenager to swoop in and save her from that misery without being caught is almost unbelievable.

She lays her head on my shoulder and continues her story. I just hold onto her, hoping there is an end to the misery in sight. It pains me to think of her hurt, used, and damaged. She is the strongest person I know, and for this world to have brought her to her knees, makes me want to both weep and battle to the ends of the Earth on her behalf.

"There was a tear in the window covering that they used to black out the window in the room that I was in," she continues. "Evan saw me and the next thing I remember is him carrying me through the house and to his car. There were drugs scattered all over the living room and their bodies were on the couch and the floor, motionless. I asked later and he said they overdosed. He took me back to Sharon, and I never had to leave her house again."

"So why do you think he killed them?" I ask.

"Because he told me he was the one who gave them the hot dose," she says. "He cleaned me up and called his mom. I remember her making phone calls before social services and the police came to the house. All I ever told them, though, was there were drugs in the house and I was with Evan when we came home and found them dead. I never moved from Sharon's house after that and we never spoke of it again."

She picks up her phone and examines the screen before looking back at me. "So yes, I love Evan," she explains. "He saved me in every way a person could be saved, and I'll forever be thankful for his bravery that day. But the only person I'm in love with is you, Lakin."

I cradle her face in my hands, wiping away any remaining tears. "I'm sorry," I tell her. "I'm sorry that happened to you and I'm sorry it wasn't me who saved you. I promise you, though, I will never let your heart hurt again. I promise you everything I have."

She pulls the back cover off her phone, revealing the love token I gave her. She throws the phone on to the bed and holds the charm out for me to hold. Campbell then takes her necklace off and replaces her forget-me-not charm with the one I gave her.

"I can't promise you everything," she says before placing my hand back onto her heart, "but I can promise you this." She smiles and kisses me deeply, twisting love and passion together and pouring it into our kiss.

"I won't ever be able to let you go," I say between kisses. "I'm stealing your forever."

I flip her over and pin her to the bed. Holding her hands above her head, I bend down and lick along her neck. "You know what I want, don't you?" I ask.

I rise up to see her smile and she pushes me to stand before her. I offer my hand and she accepts it. "I want that, too," she says with a grin.

She slides her feet into her shoes and grabs her purse. "Then let's go make it legal."

I grab her hand and pull her toward the door before she can change her mind. Before the night is over, this woman will be my wife, and I will forever be the only one who gets to save her.

Carly

The sound of the shower running wakes me up, and immediately I know I'll be paying for whatever I drank last night. I attempt to open my eyes, but my body revolts against the sensory overload of my surroundings. The sunlight peeking through the curtains forces my eyes closed again and makes my pounding head throb even worse. My throat burns as if I've swallowed sandpaper and my stomach rumbles in protest.

Slightly cracking open one eye, I find my savior...a bottle of water. I slowly wiggle to the edge of the bed and reach for the plastic bottle. The liquid hits my lips, and it's warm and stale, but at this moment, it is the best damn water on the planet. Guzzling until I finish the last drop, I then lightly place the empty bottle back on the nightstand and wait for the dehydration to ease. Already I feel better, still hungover, but better.

I want nothing more than to go back to sleep and make this morning start over again a few hours from now, but then I see a pair of jeans on the floor beside the bed. Those aren't my jeans; those aren't any of the girls' jeans. Oh, my God, they are men's jeans. I take a better look around the room and realize this isn't even my hotel room. I lift the covers and take a mental appraisal of my apparel. Panties...check, collared button-up shirt that doesn't belong to me and smells like men's cologne...check.

"Oh, sweet baby Jesus, I'm a ho," I whisper to myself as I clamp the duvet back down around my body. The water turns off in the bathroom and I scramble out of bed to find my clothes and get the hell out of the hotel room before my host makes his appearance and I have to endure an awkward morning-after that no one over the age of twenty-five should have to endure.

I dash around the room, finding piece after piece of clothing and shoes. I just need to locate my purse and I can skulk out of here, committing myself to the walk of shame. The handles are poking out from under the armchair in the corner of the room. I bend down to grab it, so I can make a run for it.

"Wow, that's a view I wouldn't mind seeing every morning," a smooth voice drawls. My body stills, wishing like hell I had the magic power of invisibility. I quickly try to think of what to say…what to do. Maybe I could make a run for it and hope I'm at least in the correct hotel. That would be horrible walking the strip or hailing a taxi in a man's shirt and black lacy boy shorts.

Oh, my God. I'm giving this guy a full peek at my ass right now. I whip around and reach for the hem of the shirt to pull it down as far as it will go to cover my ass. As mortifying as this situation is, the sensation of throwing up kicks in as soon as I lay eyes on the man on the other side of the room. He smells like heaven, and looks like a tempting Greek god. His hair is a wet mess and a towel is tightly wrapped around his waist, revealing a buffet of tattoos that I probably explored in detail last night. "Jen is going to kill me," I stammer as I nervously shift around to cover my legs.

"No worries, baby doll. What happens in Vegas stays in Vegas," Royce says with a wicked grin.

"Except herpes, that shit follows you home," I sarcastically spit out.

The gorgeous lead singer plops himself down on the bed, completely unconcerned with flashing me his manhood. "You weren't too concerned about that last night," he says, running his fingers through his wet hair.

My eyes wander around the room, desperately trying to look anywhere but at the impressive piece of maleness before me. "Can you please cover that thing up, and turn around so I can get dressed?" I ask him nervously.

"Seriously?" he scowls.

"Yes!" I screech. "I am so humiliated right now. My ex-husband didn't even see me naked; I'm certainly not going to let some random one-night stand see me."

"Well that explains a lot," he says, rolling his eyes and turning around.

As soon as I know he's not looking, I strip out of his shirt and hastily put on my clothes from last night. "What is that supposed to mean?" I ask.

"Why you came looking for me." His eyes slide to mine and his stare makes me want to melt. I resist that enticement and instead try to gather some shred of my dignity.

"Look, I don't know for sure what happened last night. Judging from my appearance this morning, I have a pretty good guess. Nonetheless, I would appreciate it if we could forget about it and never mention it to anyone." I throw my handbag over my shoulder and reach out to shake his hand.

"You're fucking with me, right?" he asks with a chuckle.

I look down at my outstretched hand. "I don't really know what's customary after sleeping with a stranger. I'm just trying to be polite." I retract my hand and let it rest at my side, slightly offended by his demeanor and foul language.

"Do you really not remember what we did last night?" he asks. "You only had two drinks at the bar." He has a somewhat whimsical grin on his face like he's amused by seeing me squirm.

"Yeah, well, I don't drink often," I sigh, getting frustrated with him, myself, and the entire encounter. "I get that this is a regular occurrence for you, but this morning-after chitchat is really uncomfortable for me. I'd really like to just leave and forget this ever happened, and I really don't want anyone else to know who I spent the evening with either. This is very embarrassing."

His smile fades and he gives me a curt nod. "Because I'm the immature man-slut, right. That's what you think of me, too." He's not asking; he's simply stating. I can see I've noticeably hurt his feelings.

He stands and readjusts his towel to cover himself up and moves past me toward the door.

"Royce, I didn't mean for that to come out the way it did," I say, hustling to catch up to him.

"I think that's exactly what you meant, but don't worry about it. I've been a lot of people's one night mistake." He opens the door and motions for me to leave. "Your secret is safe with me." His voice is monotone and flat, his eyes fixed straight ahead, not acknowledging me.

I stand, just looking at him, trying to gauge his true feelings about everything, but I can read absolutely nothing. He's completely turned off his emotions toward me. That playful Royce I saw just five minutes ago is long gone. I exhale loudly and step into the hallway.

"Well, thank you I guess," I tell him. I catch him off guard and the surprise is evident on his face.

"What are you thanking me for?" he asks, his brow scrunched. "For agreeing to forget we hung out last night so your friends won't know."

I open my mouth to explain, but he speaks and I immediately stifle my words. He moves into the hallway, with no regard for his lack of clothing. "Or maybe you're thanking me for holding your hair for you when you threw up in front of a group of tourists on the strip last night after those nasty nachos."

I shake my head in disbelief, and he nods that I did, in fact, make a spectacle of myself, in public no less. "You could even thank me for buying you a lap dance at the strip club we went to last night. Oh yeah, it happened."

He has continued to walk toward me and I'm now pinned between his massive arms and the wall behind me. My heart is pounding and I can hear myself breathing. He leans into me, placing his lips close to my ear, and all I can think is how great sleeping with him would have been and it's a shame I can't remember it.

"Whatever you want to thank me for, Carly," he whispers, "don't worry about thanking me for fucking you. As much as I would love to, and as much as you begged for it, I'm not the type of guy to take advantage of someone."

He turns and walks back into his room, leaving me panting against the wall. "No matter what you think of me, I'm not that big of an asshole," he adds before slamming the door.

I stand in the hall for a moment to collect my bearings. So not only did I drink way more than my body could handle last night, I puked in public, attended and enjoyed myself at a strip club, begged to sleep with the person who was taking care of me, and then insulted him after reviving me from my bender. Great! My cheeks flush with embarrassment. I'm a grown woman with a child and in the middle of a divorce, and I behaved like a twenty-one-year-old on spring break. Selfie pictures and film clips on social media sites would make this misadventure complete.

I quickly walk to the elevator, step inside, and push the button for my floor. Digging into my purse, I find my phone and begin my scavenger hunt through my photo gallery for evidence of my evening with Royce. Sure enough, there are pictures of the two of us all over town. Margaritaville, the fountains at the Bellagio, the roller coaster, and singing with the piano guy at the New York

New York; even pictures with groups of very attractive women. My guess would be the strippers he mentioned.

The thing I notice in all of the pictures, though, is I'm smiling…he's smiling. No matter what my preconceived notions about Royce were, he made me feel comfortable enough to spend the evening with him, and it wasn't the alcohol. We looked like friends enjoying each other, and if I hadn't let my mouth completely mess it up, we would probably be enjoying each other right now.

I close out the pictures and bring my home screen back up to see the multiple missed calls from Vivian and Jen. Numerous text messages wanting to know where I am, and if the Russian mob has kidnapped me and I need Liam Neeson to rescue me. Yeah, that one was Jen.

The elevator doors slide open and I quickly shoot off a text that I'm fine and I'll meet them for breakfast as planned. I finally make it to my hotel room and relax into my $200 a night king size bed. My eyes are still tired and my body aches, but my mind won't turn off enough to rest. Instead, I scan through the pictures of my previous evening. I look more alive and free in those images than I have felt in several years. I can't stop staring at Royce and feel bad for treating him the way I did.

I rub my hands down my face, even though my mother routinely warned me that such an action would pull at my skin and cause wrinkles. It does little to relieve the stress I feel. So I sigh deeply and do the only thing I know will help. I find the number I'm looking for and send the only words I can say.

I'm sorry.

Campbell

I struggled to pull myself away from Lakin this morning. Our bed was a cocoon of warmth and love no one should have to leave, but if I don't make it to breakfast this morning with the girls, there will be hell to pay.

Last night was one of the hardest and best of my life. Sharing my story with Lakin was so frightening. Other than Sharon and Evan, no one knows about all of it, not even the girls. Lakin was right though, if we were going to take that step, he needed to know all of me, the good and the bad. His reaction, the way he made me feel worthy, only makes me love him even more. My fear of losing everything is fading and Lakin has replaced that fear with hope…a hope for what could be.

However, I'm not ready to tell the girls what Lakin and I did last night. Even though we are here for Jen's bachelorette party, the wedding still a few months away, and Lakin and I agreed to keep it a secret until it was all over. For me, the heart we had tattooed on my ring finger is enough of a reminder of our new life together.

I kissed his temple, left him a sweet love note, and slipped out the door without waking him this morning. Maybe if I just order toast or something else equally quick, I could be back in our bed before he even notices I was gone.

When I see Jen and Vivian in the booth already, my optimism for a fast breakfast meeting diminishes. Then when I see Carly stumble to the booth, ragged and hungover, all hope is lost.

"Good lord, what happened to you?" Jen asks Carly as we both slide into the booth. I feel for her, but I'm glad those questions aren't aimed in my direction.

Carly takes a small sip of the water in front of her and then lays her head back on the cushion of the booth, looking up at the ceiling. "Royce took me around town and my liver may never recover," she says.

"How did this happen?" Vivian asks. "We called several times after dinner, no one ever answered. I thought you were going to a show."

Carly turns her head to me, pleading with me to step in, but I remain quiet. I don't have a lie to cover the evening for the both of us, so I let her flail in the wind on her own. When I say nothing, Carly throws me to the wolves.

"We were, but Campbell ditched me. I was by myself at the hotel bar when Royce found me. We just hung out. We had fun. I wouldn't mind spending more time with him. I don't see why you hate him so much," she tells Jen.

Aaaannd the atomic bomb detonates and the mushroom cloud now hovers above Jen's head.

"Royce! Hung out with Royce!" Jen squeals, her voice taking on a decibel level that only dogs could decipher. She then turns her narrowed eyes to me. "This is your fault. If you guys had gone to the show like you were supposed to, she never would have been pulled into his man-whore trap. What in the world was so important that you abandoned Carly and possibly exposed her to a life of a rock star tramp?"

"Whoa, whoa, whoa," Vivian interrupts. "Jen, you need to settle down a tad. Carly is a big girl and can spend time with whomever she wants. Campbell doesn't need to babysit her."

"It was fine, Jen," Carly chimes in. "We had a good time and he was a perfect gentleman. If anything, I was mean to him and hurt his feelings, which was entirely unwarranted."

Jen huffs and takes a drink of her orange juice. "Don't sweat it; that man has no feelings."

"Be nice, Jen, he may prove you wrong someday and you don't eat crow very well," Vivian warns.

"Yeah, and I fart rainbows and ride on unicorns," Jen jokes sarcastically. She turns to Carly and points her finger at her in a stern manner that demands attention. "Let's just not let this little friendship be a regular occurrence. That man will do nothing but string you along and break your heart. I've seen him do it tons of times, and I refuse to let him treat one of my friends that way."

Carly throws her hands up in surrender. I think more from lack of energy from her hangover, than her being convinced of Royce's negative attributes. She is appeasing her, so the conversation can shift in a different direction, and I don't blame her one bit.

If I thought it would help with Jen's opinion of him, I might have stepped in and spoke up for Royce, but I know better. Actions speak louder than words with Jen, and he has shown her no reason to believe in his virtue.

I've known Royce longer than Jen has, and yes, he flings himself from meaningless interlude to the next while on the road. I don't think the man has ever had an actual girlfriend. He's a big kid who finds humor in the most immature and ridiculous situations; he can be absolutely infuriating.

However, there is a side to him that Jen has never seen. He can be the sweetest guy with a huge heart, who would help anyone he could. Most of the money he's made he's given to his family, but Jen doesn't want to hear any of that. To her, he'll always be the front man of Absolution who can't keep it in his pants.

"What exactly did you do last night?" Vivian inquires, interrupting my thoughts.

I try to stall, so when a waitress comes by, I grab her and ask for a menu. She politely tells me it's a buffet and I can just go get whatever I would like, but if I have a special drink order, she could take care of it for me. *Great, now I look like I'm stalling.*

"You said it was soooo important. What could be more important that Cirque du Soleil?" Carly adds.

I take a drink of my water and blurt out the first thing that comes to mind.

"I ate something that upset my stomach and had diarrhea. I didn't want to be stuck in a show when another round hit me," I explain. Judging from the looks on their faces, I picked a winner. Nothing like a fecal incident to halt a conversation immediately.

"I guarantee there were no rainbows being shit in that bathroom," Jen laughs, which earns a harsh look from Vivian and a mild slap on the arm.

"Are you feeling better?" Vivian asks concerned.

"I'm fine," I say.

"Thank you for not including me," Carly adds. "You can ditch me any time, if loose bowels are the cause. I'm glad you're feeling better, though. We have a big night, beer poos are not allowed."

Jen rolls her eyes and laughs. "We are in Vegas and there are no kids in the near vicinity, cussing is allowed, Car. Beer shits, the terms is called beer shits."

Jen then turns back to me. "But she is right, no beer shits allowed."

I nod and hold up my two fingers for the Boy's Scout's pledge.

Everyone laughs, and just like that, the tension at the table evaporates. We are once again four friends, four sisters who are here to enjoy each other. Complications and drama of home, forgotten. Men, relationships, kids, jobs, everything put on hold in order to enjoy the moment. Enjoy each other.

"So what's on the agenda?" I ask.

"Shopping, the pool, sleeping, and then primping for a night on the town," Jen says excitedly. "Vegas will never be the same when we get done with it. Tonight will be epic!"

The three of us look to each other and then to Jen. Excitement, worry, apprehension, all passing between us.

"We better start scraping together bail money now," Carly announces under her breath. Jen stares at her, thinking momentarily before a huge grin splits across her face.

"You bet your sweet ass!"

Royce

After buttoning up my dress shirt, styling my mop of a hairstyle, and spraying my favorite cologne, I spend the next five minutes waiting for the guys and staring at the text Carly sent me this morning.

"I'm sorry," one of the most powerful phrases in the human language. With two simple words, the wounds she inflicted have begun to heal. She pissed me off royally this morning, but after having a deep conversation with my Sally doll, I've come to realize she just reacted poorly to an uncompromising situation.

A pounding on my door breaks the silence in my room, and I hustle to answer it.

"Are you ready to tear shit up tonight?" our drummer, John, asks as the rest of the guys filter into my room. I stuff my wallet and phone into my pocket and tuck Sally under my arm.

"Is that really a question you need to ask?" I ask them with a huff.

Casen pulls the blow up doll out of my grasp. "I can't, dude. No way. You cannot bring this thing along. The girls will be going with us, and I know Jen will have a fucking fit."

I laugh and pull the doll away from him. "All the more reason to bring her along," I say before marching out of the hotel room to the elevators. The footsteps behind me and the door closing tell me the resistance is over; Sally has officially become our party mascot. I at least thought ahead enough to dress her in a tasteful outfit for the evening.

The metal doors open and we all step into the elevator. "Jen is seriously going to kill you," John whispers to me as we take the ride to the lobby. I ignore his warning, although I know he's absolutely right; I need to prepare for battle.

When the doors open, we walk past a row of slots and find ourselves in the lobby. A circle of smiles greet our arrival, but it doesn't take long for one grin to disappear. "Fuck no, not happening," Jen exclaims. "Casen, rein your boy in," she demands.

All of the girls are dressed in the usual bachelorette paraphernalia of penis necklaces and tiaras while Jen fashions the bride sash across her chest. I personally think Sally fits right in.

I hoist Sally up on my shoulder and bounce her like she's just made the winning shot in a championship game. "She's our wedding mascot," I insist. "Sally will be our ticket to VIP sections."

The girls, with the exception of Jen, laugh. I recognize Carly's laugh instantly and I find myself yearning to hear it again.

"More like our ticket to videos and pictures gone viral," Campbell jokes.

I grab ahold of the penis necklace that dangles from Carly's neck. "If you girls get to wear phallic jewelry in public, then Sally should get to come along."

"Fine, but she rides in the trunk or on the roof," Jen growls.

Now that our disagreement is settled, we head toward the exit. The noise of the Vegas strip is exciting. The energy of the atmosphere infects my body and causes a vibration within my system. I find Carly in our crowd and navigate to her.

Casen hails cabs for us and I rush to get to her so I can share a cab with her, but the girls crowd me out. Instead, I'm stuck with my bandmates, John and Seiger, and Lakin.

We all pile into the cab, and I make sure there is enough room for Sally, as I refuse to follow Jen's trunk rule.

"Buckle up for safety," I say once we smoosh in. The comment garners me a stern, unappreciated look from them all. "Oh come on you guys, this is supposed to be a fun night, don't be asses."

"Where to, guys?" the cabbie asks before looking in his rearview mirror. His Eastern European accent is so thick I can barely comprehend his question.

"Tallywacker's, we are in the mood for a little punany bread," I say with the utmost seriousness.

Lakin snaps his head to me, like he can't believe what I've just said. When a broad smile appears on my face, he just shakes his head at my level of immaturity.

"I know no such place," the driver call's back. "You get guys and girls there?" he asks.

When we don't answer right away, he looks back at us and sees Sally. His brow reaches into his receding hairline and nods his head in an unspoken understanding.

"I know just where to take you boys," he says before whipping the cab into traffic.

The four of us look back and forth to each other in confusion.

"You like men too, or just the women?" he asks. "I can find cheap, cheap rates for you. Just tell me what you like."

"Ummm," Seiger begins to say, uncomfortable with our new possible destination as opposed to Fremont Street as planned. "We...um," he stutters again, unable to spit out any recognizable complete sentence.

John sees the grand opportunity to fuck with Seiger and I give him the nod to pounce.

"We prefer the women, but my friend here," John says, pointing to Seiger, "likes the men, but they must be midgets."

"What?" Seiger exclaims. "No. No. No. No. No. I like the women. I like the women," he insists.

I sneak a peek over at Lakin, and he's trying to hide his laugh in his hand.

"You no worry," the cabbie says reassuringly. "I find you good little guy."

"No little guy," Seiger says, narrowing his eyes at us. "We want to go to Fremont, sir."

We try to maintain our composure, because the second we laugh the joke will be over. Lakin is desperately trying to keep it together, but with every passing second he struggles more and more.

"Fremont, may be hard and more money," the guys says. "How much you pay? The tip counts you know," he adds with a wink.

Aaaannd that does it, Lakin snorts and breaks into hysterics. His laugh is contagious and I have to duck behind the Sally doll to conceal my laughter.

"No men, no women, just take us to Fremont Street," Seiger demands.

"Okay, okay," the cabbie resigns. "You change your mind, just find me. I hook you up."

Within minutes, our cabbie has us parked on the street that will lead us on the short walk to Fremont. Up ahead the crowd has overtaken the area to watch a band playing on the main stage and onlookers stare as people fly above the crowd on the zip line.

A pissed off Seiger bursts out of the cab slamming the door behind him. He catches Sally's head in the car door, popping the plastic. She deflates immediately, air hissing in the back of the cab, with no way of saving her.

I jump out and race around to see her flattened head hang out of the car door.

"Dude! There's no reason to take out your anger on Sally," I say as the cabbie drives away with her head flapping in the wind.

"Yeah, she was an innocent bystander in all of this," John teases.

"I betcha that cabbie can get you a new one," Seiger says. "You guys are assholes."

His lack of humor toward the situation makes us laugh even harder. "Sorry, man," I tell him. "We couldn't pass up the chance."

He crosses his arms across his body, sulking. "You're fucking hilarious," he steams.

Lakin pulls out his phone and sends a text to the rest of the crew. Hopefully, we can catch up with them. "Come on," he says as he puts his phone back in his pocket. "I'll buy you all the first round. It will only take a couple of drinks for that ride to be funny, Seiger."

Lakin was absolutely right. Three drinks in and the cab ride was an epic story, which Seiger felt free to share with anyone who would listen at the bar.

Somehow, amongst the crowd, we managed to find the other carload of our group, but I didn't get to spend any of our time out with Carly. Jen made sure to keep the girls partitioned away from us, and it became a look but don't touch situation in regards to Carly. After my buzz began to wear off and I realized none of my efforts were going to be aimed at the one girl I actually wanted to talk to, I caught the bus back to the strip.

The girls left long before I did, and none of the guys were ready to leave, so the bus ride home is a lonely one. Although the bus would take me all the way to my hotel, I decide to hop off on one side of the strip and enjoy the long trek back to the hotel. I could use the fresh air to think about how I'm going to get another chance with Carly.

I make it all the way to the Bellagio before I stop to see the water display. The crowds have thinned, so finding a spot along the stone edging in the middle is easy to find. I lean on the cooled rock and wait, and wait.

After several minutes of no show, I look around for any clues as to why nothing is happening. Looking down the edging, I notice Carly leaning against the stone just as I am, a mere fifty feet away.

She hasn't noticed me.

I close the gap between us and scoot in close to her, staring out at the water, when I finally reach her.

"Did I miss a memo or something?" I ask.

"By about two hours," she responds without missing a beat, making me think she did see me and just chose not to acknowledge me.

She turns and smiles at me, which puts my fears to rest. "I googled it. They turn the fountains off at midnight. We'll have to catch it tomorrow before we leave."

I zone in on her use of the word we, and I absolutely love the sound. "We'll have to do that," I say, adding my own we into the conversation.

She nods and turns her back to the water, leaning against the rocks. "What happened to Sally? I noticed she didn't make it to the bar, but I didn't get a chance to ask."

"It's a long story," I laugh. "Let's just say the old girl has been laid to rest."

"Ah, I see."

I look out at the water and let silence take over the moment.

"I really am sorry about this morning," she finally says. "I enjoyed being with you last night, and I hope it wasn't the last time."

A sense of relief overtakes me. She says the exact words I was hoping for. Carly is a force I would struggle to stay away from. So to hear her say that she would like to see me again, even if it's in a non-romantic capacity, well, it's something. I struggle with my need to push the envelope, push her toward something more with me.

Throwing caution to the wind, I grab her waist and slide her body in-between mine and the rocks, caging her in. Pushing her silky brunette hair away from her face, I cradle her face in my hands. Leaning in, I lightly rub my lips against hers, not kissing, just tempting, teasing her. When I finally hear the begging whimper I'm looking for, I plunge ahead, devouring her mouth.

She feels just as good as I hoped she would, a sensation I could come to crave. I could spend every day for the rest of my life touching these lips, and it wouldn't be enough.

I finally pull away and tuck a loose strand behind her ear. "You won't be getting rid of me anytime soon."

Two Weeks Later

Campbell

Lying by omission is still lying.

That's what I've been told at least. But there is no malice or deceit in my omission; it has been a necessity. The girls can't know I'm married, and so far Lakin and I have done an impressive job at hiding it. Everyone is still adjusting to the idea of he and I being in a relationship, so I don't think the news of our marriage would be well received.

While I spend a great deal of my days with the bands or the kids at the foundation, my nights are devoted to my husband. For now, I've maintained my own apartment, but I'm not really living there; Lakin's apartment is my home. The secrecy of our situation has been something I have found comforting. It's special and it's mine.

My only other focus right now is someone I see as a younger version of myself…Leah. Carly agreed to show up at the foundation today to meet her. If they click, then she will look into moving forward with getting approval as a foster parent.

Carly steps into Vivian's office fifteen minutes earlier than I am expecting. She looks apprehensive and timid, and I completely understand. She's preparing to possibly step across hot coals, and is hopeful she doesn't end up scorched. I wish I could reassure her that she'll safely make it to the other side, but that's not a promise I can make.

"Hey," she says. "I just got back from my lawyer's office and I didn't have time to go home, so I thought early was better than late."

I stand up from the couch to greet her and offer as much support as I can. "It's no problem; Leah is here already. She's talking to some kids in one of the conference rooms."

Carly fidgets, each of her hands wrestling the other. "What should we do, wait here for her or should I go out to the commons area? I guess I'm not sure what to do."

"Car, you need to relax and breathe a bit, girl," I tell her. "Leah is wearing some cut off jean shorts, a purple tank, and has a bright pink backpack. You can't miss her. Go out to the activities area and hang out with the kids; when she comes out, I'll find you and introduce you."

She nods, closing her eyes and breathing deeply. "I'm just worried," she finally says.

I tilt my head, looking for further clarification. Nervous, anxious, yes, but worried? I can't imagine what she would be worried about.

"I don't want to mess it up," she explains. "If she needs a home and I'm a good fit, then I want to help. What if she doesn't like me? What if I'm not strong enough to pull this off?"

"How could anyone not like you? You are the most selfless, most compassionate person I know. Leah, isn't going to like you; she's going to love you, just like I do."

I mean every word I tell her, and apparently they provide the courage she needs because she smiles and turns to leave the room.

I'm tempted to go with her, be her bridge, her crutch to meet the kids at the foundation, but I know better. She needs to gather her own bravery, otherwise the kids will see right through her and she will be of no use to any of them, including Leah.

I force myself to wait fifteen minutes, when I know the group discussion will be minutes from concluding, before stepping into the hallway. I'm hoping to catch Leah in the hall as she exits the conference room, but when I arrive, Carly is standing outside, the door to the room wide open.

I step around her to see Leah is still talking with the group, and I know exactly what she is telling them, the stories Carly just heard. How she would purposely wet her pants because she thought no one would want her so they would have to send her back to her mother. How her mother would leave her home alone with no food for days at a time when she was on a bender. How by the time she finally realized her mother couldn't be a real mother for her, her likelihood of finding a permanent home was slim to none. She was destined to be a statistic, and she hoped she would beat the odds. Carly heard every gut-wrenching word of Leah's story, and for the first time, I was scared Carly would walk away from her.

I see the mascara is running down her cheeks, and I ask her if she is okay. She ignores the question and hastily brushes the tears away from her face.

"Tell me what I need to do," she says, her voice shaking with emotion.

Initially, I'm perplexed by her question. "To do what, Car? Be a foster parent?" I ask.

She looks back into the room where Leah is now gathering up her backpack, clears her throat, and then squares her shoulders toward me.

"No," she says confidently. "To adopt her."

Carly

I haven't seen Royce since Vegas, but I haven't been able to get that kiss out of my mind. We have texted back and forth a few times, but he has been busy recording and I have been wrapped up in work and getting to know Leah.

I must be half insane to travel down the adoption road, but there was just something about her that spoke to me and I couldn't turn my back on her.

It's like I see Campbell in her. I want to give this girl a life that my friend had to make for herself. I may not even be approved to adopt Leah, but I can't help but want to try.

Needless to say, this dinner tonight was not high on my priority list. I wanted to go home after work, curl up on the couch with Liv, and watch Disney movies to her heart's content.

This group dinner was Jen's idea. The wedding is just around the corner and she feels the need to bring us together as much as possible to turn bridezilla loose.

Trying to be a good friend, we agreed to come over anyways.

Liv and I unload out of the car and make our way up the steps to Casen and Jen's massive house. Bright, beautiful flowers line the walkway to the front porch, most of which I have to rescue before Liv gets her hands on them.

Spotting us through the drapes, Jen answers the door before we have a chance to knock and pulls us both into the house.

I look around at baby gate central and I can't help but laugh. Jen is the most free-spirited, adventurous person I know, yet Ryker's birth has somehow transformed her into that helicopter momma bear we all joke about.

"My goodness, Jen," I laugh. "We are going to have to step over a baby gate to get in any room or hallway in this house." I look to the wall next to me, which has outlet covers in the holes, and continue my teasing. "Ryker isn't even two feet tall, how is he going to reach an outlet that's halfway up the wall? Is he part of the Incredibles' cast and you just haven't told us?"

"Shush, you can never be too careful, and if I'm being honest, Casen was in charge of the baby proofing; he just got a little carried away."

I nod, knowing she is absolutely lying through her teeth. Yes, Casen is extremely protective of his son and their daughter Abby, but this is the workings of Jen. She just doesn't want to come under fire for it, so she instead opts to throw her fiancé under the bus. We've all done it a million times; I'm just surprised Jen wouldn't fess up to it.

Liv runs through the house in search of Emma and Grace, while Jen grabs my hand and leads me down a back hallway. I hear laughter and glasses clinking together in the opposite direction, so I offer my best 'what the heck' look to Jen as she passes by the direction of the noise and crowd.

"The party's that way. Am I missing something here, or did I do something wrong that deserves a private lashing?" The latter is entirely possible. Jen's stress level is out of hand as the wedding approaches. We are all covering our asses, hoping the days fly by. November can't get here quick enough.

She looks around my shoulder and ducks back into her bedroom. "No, this isn't wedding related."

"Okaaayyy," I draw out.

"I know you and Royce shared some gross, sloppy kiss in Vegas—"

"Hey," I cut her off. "It was a nice kiss. He and I have been talking. I really think you would like him if you gave him a chance."

"Yeah, well, Casen just told me Royce is coming tonight and he's bringing a girl. I wanted to give you the heads up."

"What!" I screech. I had no idea he would be here and, therefore didn't do a decent or even adequate job with my appearance, and then to hear he's bringing someone…dagger to the stomach. I should be looking top notch; make him regret his decision to ever flaunt another woman in front of me. "Darn it, Jen. What a jerk!"

"Darn it, really?" she says, narrowing her eyes at me. "I think this deserves a little more profanity, a good old 'fuck that douchebag' fits the situation. I warned you what kind of guy he is."

"Well, what do I do?" I ask, my frustration reflected in my voice. "I don't want to be the poor sap they laugh about when they leave. I'm so embarrassed."

How could I have been so stupid? Of course, Royce would be bringing a date, probably some hot twenty-year-old with tits under her chin and legs for days. I could never compete. I don't know why I thought I could. Still, that is so rude to bring her here in front of me without bothering to tell me he wasn't interested in me. Jen's right, he's an asshole.

"I'll tell you what we're going to do. We're going to doll you up, you're going to ignore him, and he'll be sorry he ever played with your delicate feelings."

I exhale loudly. While I would like to fix myself up a bit, I have no intentions of ignoring him. Nope, I'll call him out and be super nice to the tart he brings. I can be the bigger person, and that will be more powerful than any silent treatment can be. I won't let him get under my skin. I won't let myself be hurt by this. Jack's done enough of that to last a lifetime.

Jen has already left my side and is rummaging through her closet. With her job, she gets samples in every size and she tucks them away as gifts for us. I always thought it was not all that thoughtful of her to re-gift hand-me-downs that she doesn't want, but in this moment, my goodness, I'm super thankful for something decent in my size in her closet. Lord knows I couldn't borrow anything of hers, and the drab outfit I'm sporting isn't going to make the cut.

"Here, try this," she says, throwing a cute strappy dress at me before heading back into her closet. "I think I have some boots that will match."

I undress and throw on the outfit, and when the boots come flying at me, I grab those and slide my feet into them as well. Jen finally reappears and examines me closely.

"Head to my bathroom; we need to touch up your makeup and hair a bit," she demands.

I follow her into her expansive bathroom fit for a queen. She scrambles around me, gathering makeup in my perfect shades, turning on a hair straightener, and assembling a barrage of brushes.

She pulls the ponytail holder from my hair and feverously runs the strands between the steam of the flat iron. Once every piece is in place, she begins working on my makeup.

"I can't wait to make him suffer," she says under her breath, a comment that makes me pause. I grab her hand, pushing it down by her side.

"Are you doing this to make me feel better about myself or to hurt Royce?" I ask. "You didn't want me with him anyways."

She moves the blush brush back up to my cheek and shrugs her shoulder. "Same difference," she says nonchalantly.

I take the brush from her hand and step away. "I appreciate what you're doing, but I think I'll be fine. I'm just going to go out there. I don't need to waste my time on a guy who had no intention of pursuing anything anyway."

Her nose scrunches in misunderstanding. "What are you talking about? I thought you wanted to make him wish he were never born."

"It's his loss, but thanks."

I hand her the blush brush and walk past her. I hear her throw it on the bathroom counter and she quickly follows behind me. Soon as we are walking toward the deck where the rest of our adult party-goers are. In the kitchen, we are met with warm welcomes, and of course, hugs from Vivian.

"Where have you been, ladies?" Casen asks before offering us both a beer.

"Oh, you know, just girl talk," I say, accepting the cold bottle and taking a swig, trying to fade into the crowd. He gives Jen a knowing look and huffs with a smile. Jen narrows her eyes at him and shoos him away. Casen picks Ryker up from his high chair and takes him outside, leading the others to the back deck. When the doors open, I can hear the chatter and laughter of the kids playing in the backyard.

I turn my feet to follow the crowd when the doorbell rings. I look around the girls, and Jen states exactly what I'm thinking. "The douche patrol is here." Well, not exactly what I'm thinking.

She briskly walks to the door and hastily pulls it open. "Welcome, come on in. The guys are out back," she says, overly unenthusiastic and monotone. She immediately turns and leaves Royce and his guest on the steps.

"Well, thank you for that warm welcome, Jen," I hear Royce say. "I didn't know how I was going to make it through the day without seeing your friendly face." The sarcasm drips from his voice.

He and his guest finally step into the house and my heart sinks. He is just as gorgeous as I remember him, and she is the perfect arm candy, adorable and tiny enough to fit in my pocket. Her brunette curls bounce just above her shoulders and her smile is bright and cheery. My jealousy spikes when I see him put his hand on her back to guide her further into the space, but I try to taper it down.

Jen notices my discomfort and grabs my arm, pulling me toward her. "I would offer to kick her in the cooch but I'm afraid I would lose a shoe, and I'm fairly attached to my strappy sandals," Jen whispers in my ear.

"Stop it," I hush back at her. "She looks really nice, like someone we would hang out with if the situation were different."

Vivian rushes forward to offer a better greeting, shaking their hands and walking with them to our little group.

"Hi Royce, good to see you again," I say when they finally reach us. I try my hardest to be pleasant, and when Royce returns my smile, I know I've pulled off the ruse.

"This is Hannah," he says as she offers a shy wave.

"Sorry, I'm a little nervous meeting you all. Royce speaks so highly of everyone. I didn't want to disappoint," Hannah says.

Don't I feel like a shit? I should be angry at Royce for never saying he was dating someone, not this poor girl who was just as clueless as I was.

"I thought you guys would get along wonderfully. I guess I didn't take into account the Jen monster." He points his thumb toward Jen.

I smile and, thankfully, Campbell steps in and offers Hannah a drink. Vivian folds an arm through hers and together they pull the sweet girl to the deck where the others are.

"Let's go, Jen," Campbell shouts from the kitchen.

"I'm watching you," she tells Royce, backpedaling into the kitchen. "One wrong move and I'll have you out on your ass."

Royce doesn't answer; he simply salutes her before bringing his attention back to me.

"What's all this about?" he asks, waving his hands around my face. "You look...different. Good," he stutters, "just different."

"I made the mistake of allowing Jen to do my makeup," I explain with an embarrassed smile. "Hannah seems nice," I add, trying to change the subject.

He laughs and scratches the facial hair that lines his chin. "She's a bit of a pain in my ass, but I'm kind of stuck with her," he finally says. He pulls me close to him and rubs my cheek where Jen went a little wild with the blush. "I like Carly just the way she is, no additives needed," he whispers in my ear before moving past me to meet the others outside.

What in the ever-loving hell?

We hit it off, hang out, and even kiss in Vegas. We've been texting and talking since we got back, then bam! He shows up with a date, but then tells me he likes plain old me.

No thank you, I'm too old to play games. High school love triangles lost their appeal in high school. I'm happy to be his friend, and if one day he was capable, maybe more. For right now, I don't need what he's offering in my life. I have enough complication and crazy for the whole group without groupie girl drama added to the mix.

I take another drink of my beer and follow the same path as the others to the backyard. My friends have made a circle in the grass and the guys have stationed themselves around the barbecue grill. The older kids are playing on the swing set while the babies crawl in the grass and play with a small pile of toys. This is what group get-togethers always look like. There's only one major difference today; Royce and Hannah have joined us.

Instead of immediately joining my circle of girls, I hang back on the deck. Even though I've placed Royce in the friend column, I can't help but still watch his interaction with Hannah. The two of them are friendly and close, but not touchy feely, not how I would imagine Royce would be with a girlfriend. I've had years of half-assed affection from Jack, I guess I dodged a bullet by not pursuing anything with Royce.

Then suddenly, Jen's screams for Casen break through my stalking moment and all attention is focused on Jen's panic as she picks up Ryker from the grass. Tears stream down her face as fear paralyzes her. The guys rush to them, Casen leading the pack, and as I get closer, I see what the commotion is about...Ryker is choking. His little eyes are watering from trying to expel whatever is stuck in his throat, and his red face is strained from the lack of oxygen.

Before Casen even has the opportunity do anything for Ryker, Royce grabs him from Jen's arms. He turns the baby on his arm and pats hard on his back. I cringe watching, idle, useless to help. It feels like forever, but within seconds, Royce pulls him back up and swipes a finger through Ryker's mouth.

There are gasps all around when Ryker's cries pierce the silence of the moment. Royce then pulls the baby close and tenderly pats him on the back, whispering to him.

He hands him back to Jen who grabs ahold of him tightly and caresses his little head as she rocks him. He turns to Casen and hands him the small pebble that had been wedged in Ryker's throat. Everyone's jaws are hanging open in surprise. This was an extremely tense moment, and the last person anyone expected to save the day was Royce.

Casen shakes his hand. "Thank you, man," he says. He pauses, looking down at the rock in his hand. "I don't know what to say," he stammers, emotion filling his voice. "Thank you."

"I have a nephew who we lovingly refer to as the vacuum. From the age of six months to eighteen months, if it was on the floor, that kid was putting it in his mouth. My poor sister was constantly scanning the floor for anything he could get his hands on, but it didn't matter; he would find it and choke on it." Royce tries to make light of the situation, easing the tension. We all know, though, if he had not acted as fast as he had, this could have ended very badly.

Ryker's cries have softened to nothing more than ragged breaths, and Jen paces around with him as Vivian follows behind offering motherly support. She is paying no attention to Royce's family stories or his reasoning for how he knew what to do. She is focusing on her child.

My heart aches for her. Liv has never had more than an ear infection or a scraped knee; the possibility of losing her would bring me to my knees. I love all of these people so much; their pain is my pain.

Royce is still rambling on about his sisters and their kids when Jen marches up to him and bear hugs him. Ryker is smashed between the two, but she continues to hold tight to Royce's neck.

"I'll never be able to show you how thankful I am for what you did for us today," she tells him. Her voice breaks, but unlike Casen, she allows her emotion to show. "I'm so sorry for every mean thing I said to or about you."

He soothingly rubs her back before pulling way to stroke Ryker's head. "It was no big deal, really," he says before turning his attention to me. "I'm sure I'll think of something, though," he adds with a wink.

Carly

"Hurry, Liv, we are so late!" I shout from my bathroom. "Grab your shoes and jacket, and meet me at the door."

My voice echoes down the hallway, and I know the lack of response means I will find a child with neither shoes nor jacket when I finally emerge from my room. I'm supposed to be at work in thirty minutes, and I still have to take Olivia to Vivian's. I hate being late, and I think this day will prove to be one big smelly fart ready to crop dust me at every turn.

Brushing and curling the last segment of my hair, which looks like a whole colony of mice could live in, the door bells rings, distracting me from my styling mess. "Great," I mutter, throwing the brush onto the counter.

I grab my shoes and teeter back and forth from foot to foot, cinching them on. "Hurry, Liv," I shout once more as I race down the hall and through the living room to the entry door.

"Look, Jack, now's not a good time. I'm running late this morning," I say as I swing open the door and bend down to finish buckling my sandals.

"Um, sorry, wrong guy," my visitor smoothly responds, forcing my head up to meet him.

Well, crap on a cracker…Royce.

"Sorry," I say, standing and holding the door open for him. "He's been calling and showing up a lot lately now that the divorce is in full swing and getting closer to being finalized. I just assumed it would be him here to bother me."

He steps through the door, and I catch a whiff of his cologne as he passes. It's enticing enough that I find myself leaning in momentarily to take in just a little more of the inebriating smell. *Sweet baby Jesus, he's delicious.*

It's early morning; yet, he has this look that says, 'I'm a rock star, and I don't keep hours. Besides, I look good no matter the time.' I don't think he even tries to be sexy, he just is. His beard, tousled hair that can be pulled into a knot, and tattoos are the qualities that Jen, or even Campbell, would drool over, not me. However, here Royce is, and I can't seem to help myself. I want to just lick him up.

I pat my hair down and adjust my clothing, feeling somewhat self-conscious in his presence. I then give him a sideways glance that suggests an explanation for his early morning visit.

"I was recording last night with the guys and Casen said Liv left her favorite stuffed animal at their house. I volunteered to bring it over," he says nervously as he offers her elephant to me and moves further into the house. "So you're late for work, huh?" he asks, leaving me behind.

"Ugh, yes," I groan, throwing the stuffed animal on the couch and following him. "I still have to get Liv to Vivian's house. She's staying over there tonight since I have a meeting after work with the county about adopting Leah."

"If you want, I can watch her and drop her off at Vivian's house later," he suggests nonchalantly with a shrug.

I stop suddenly, contemplating his offer. "Have you ever even been around kids all by yourself?" I ask, dumbfounded that he would even offer.

He turns to look at me, a confused expression smeared across his face. "Seriously?" he asks. "I love kids. I have about a million nieces and nephews that I babysit all the time.

"You do?" I say, stunned that he is that involved with his family.

"Yeah, apparently my sisters are competing for the steel vagina award or something. I swear, as soon as one announces they're pregnant, another pipes up and tries to steal her thunder with a similar announcement. We are a family of one-uppers."

"Wow, lots of warm and fuzzies. I bet Christmases are super special," I tease.

"Really, though, I don't have anything going on today. I would be happy to help."

I look down at my watch and bite my lip as we walk into the kitchen. I don't look up until I hear Royce chuckling next to me.

"Oh, my God," I gasp as I stare down at my child who is supposed to be ready to walk out the door. Instead of her shoes and jacket on, she's standing in the middle of the kitchen with her favorite Disney princess dress and tiara on drinking from the maple syrup bottle. When she notices us, she hides the bottle behind her back and smiles a goopy grin at us.

Royce wipes the smile from his face and slowly approaches her. "You know what's cool about being a grown up, little miss?" he asks as he takes the bottle from her hands and sits down cross-legged next to her. She immediately feels at ease and takes a place next to him on the kitchen floor as she shakes her head.

I tilt my head in awe of what I'm witnessing, my little girl and this tough rocker bonding over maple syrup.

He leans in like he has a secret, and she leans in to hear it. "You don't have to hide the bottle from anyone," he tells her with a smile before taking a big chug of the syrup.

They both giggle at his playfulness, while I nearly throw up. "I can't believe you just did that!" I say incredulously. "Not even taking into account how unsanitary that was, it was just, well, gross," I add with a body shiver.

They both laugh even more at my obvious discomfort. "Go. I'll take care of her. I'll even swing back by this evening and bring dinner and a movie over."

I look back and forth between the two of them and then down at my watch. "Are you sure?"

"Absolutely! We'll make pancakes and have a princess rock concert before we go. Just leave me a car seat, please."

"Pancakes," Olivia squeals. "I need a fok n' knife," she adds, entirely leaving out the r in fork.

"Dear God, did she just say fucking knife?" he asks with a snort. "I'm not a parent, but I'm pretty sure a four-year-old with a potty mouth is frowned upon in most social circles."

"She's a little Dutchy," I defend. "Those R's get left out a lot. She is saying she needs a fork and knife."

He holds up his hand for Liv to high-five and smiles at her. "Either way, you're one kickass little munchkin. Let's get our pancake on." My heart melts a little watching the two interact together. Royce barely knows me, let alone my daughter, yet here he is stepping in to play babysitter. I'm appreciative and impressed all in one.

Liv hops up to give me a hug. "Bye, Momma," she says, wrapping her sticky hands around my legs. I reach down and kiss the top of her head before she runs back to Royce.

Royce looks to me and throws his hand up in surrender. "Bye, Mom," he chuckles and waves.

I exhale loudly. "Okay, but please be safe."

I turn my attention to Olivia who has found herself enamored by this tatted man on our kitchen hardwood. "Liv, this is Mommy's friend Royce. He's going to take you over to Grace and Emma's house," I tell her, bending down to her eye level to get her full attention. "Is that okay with you?" I ask, hoping it works out because I now have fifteen minute to get to work and it would take at least that to get to Vivian's. Royce is actually a lifesaver showing up here this morning, even if it was unexpected.

"You bet, Mom. I'm gonna be a rock chick!" she exclaims.

I roll my eyes and Royce laughs. "You," I say pointing my finger at him. "Don't corrupt my child in the brief time she's in your care."

"What!" he feigns insult. "I'm the coolest person she'll ever meet. Anything I do will only catapult her awesome rocker status at preschool next year."

"That's what I'm afraid of," I add with a hint of smile.

"Aren't you late?" he asks, tapping his thick buckle watch.

"Oh cheese and crackers, yes," I huff, standing to grab my purse off the kitchen counter. "I'll call Vivian and let her know the slight change in plan. Have a good day you guys. Love you, Liv."

I hear her shout her goodbyes and love back to me as I race into the living room and out the front door. Echoes of giggling and snorting noises reverberate through the house as I close the door shut and sprint to my car.

I turn the key in the ignition and take one last look at the house. "I must be crazy," I mumble shaking my head before putting the car into reverse and heading to work.

Royce

Olivia proved to be quite the handful, but in the best way. We had so much fun, but between breakfast, dress-up, our mini rock concert, and a few art projects, together we completely destroyed Carly's house. I had to take Liv to the Ryans' house just so I could get the place cleaned up before Carly came home and saw the mess. She would flip, and I would lose any future chance I might get at hanging out with her.

I framed the pictures Liv drew her and put them on the kitchen table, vacuumed, and dusted...the whole nine yards. Once late afternoon hit, I rushed out to get dinner and a few movies, as well as movie snacks, since I didn't know what time she would be home. I figure I would rather be here sooner rather than later.

Spreading the Chinese food takeout boxes across the table, I lay out two plates for the two of us. I don't know what she likes, or even if she likes Chinese food at all, but I went with it. I mean, who doesn't like it? Besides, I ordered just about everything on the menu, so she would have a few options.

Just as I place the movies and candy on the kitchen counter, the doorbell rings and I freeze. For a solid minute, I have a mental debate on whether or not to answer the freaking door. It could be Vivian needing something for Liv. I've technically overstayed my invitation, so it could just as easily be some nosey neighbor checking on the creepy-looking guy prowling the house.

"Oh fuck it, Grandma down the street can call the police if she doesn't like me," I say to myself, dropping everything and heading to the front door.

I open the door and am immediately met with a dirty look. *Apparently, Grandma is really a thirtysomething businessman in a suit.*

"Who the hell are you? Where's Carly?" the man asks.

"Well, hello there, pops. I'm Royce," I say, attempting to be respectful, but I can already feel this conversation spiraling downward. "Carly's not here right now. Can I help you with something?"

His lips purse at my last comment. "Who are you?" he coldly asks again. "And where is my fat bitch of a wife?"

My face heats up and my fingers ball into fists. How fucking dare Jack show up on this doorstep, and not only talk to me this way, but to be so disrespectful toward Carly. He has some fucking nerve.

I take a deep breath to calm my temper. A brawl on the front porch will definitely get the cops called, and would only hurt Carly's divorce case. So instead of my hands, I opt for my words. I am a songwriter/poet after all.

"Like I said," I say casually. "Carly's not here. But as the current guy fucking your wife, I'd be happy to let her know you stopped by," I add with a sly grin. His eyes widen, but before he can respond, I slam the door in his face. It was a lie, but it feels like a really good lie. That guy's a douche and it serves him right to think his wife isn't pining away for him, but instead is getting railed by some hot piece like me.

There is a brief moment of silence before an eruption…the calm before the storm. "How fucking dare you?" he roars. "You'll pay for that. She hasn't heard the end of this. Let her know I'll be back."

I glance out the front windows to see him race down the driveway to his car. He slams his car door and peels out into the street. I wave politely, but am met with a not so polite hand gesture.

"Asshole," I mutter as I turn and head back into the kitchen to finish dinner preparations. I barely get the candy arranged before I hear the front door open and Carly's tread through the living room. I lean against the counter, plaster a smile on my face, and wait for her to enter the kitchen, except she doesn't come into the kitchen. I wait and wait, but nothing.

I push off of the counter and follow her path of stripped off shoes, jacket, and purse down the hallway to her bedroom. Music is filtering through the house, not my music, but I'll let that slide.

When I finally reach her bedroom, I stand briefly in the open entrance and view the bundle of energetic movements before me. She has stripped down to her bra and panties and is dancing all over the room like some sort of teen dance party.

I cover my mouth to hide my smile. She is so free and happy; I don't want to interrupt. I sure as hell know I shouldn't be watching, but I can't pull myself away to walk back down the hall to where I should be.

Reaching my hand up to knock on her bedroom door, she catches sight of me in her dresser mirror. My eyes must bulge out of my head, because Carly freaks out.

"Ahhh!" she screams. "What are you doing here?" Carly immediately reaches for a pillow on her bed to shield herself with.

"I was bringing dinner over, remember?" I offer, somewhat stammering at the fact I got caught peeping on her.

"I didn't think you would already be here...in my house," she persists. "Can you please at least turn around?" she begs.

"You know, I've seen you like this before, right? It's not that big of a deal," I say, trying to put her a little more at ease. Shit, I see tits on a daily basis when the band is performing. I'm continually offered a diversified portfolio of pussy; a little bra and panties action isn't going to throw me into some tizzy.

She scowls at me and a little begging whimper escapes her lips.

Now, that does have me a little flustered. Damn, if it isn't the sexiest fucking sound I've ever heard. Carly begging is a beautiful notion, and I let the scenarios play out in my head.

"Royce!" she finally hollers sternly, gaining my attention once again.

I roll my eyes and turn around so she can get dressed. "Don't make such a big deal about this, Carly. You don't have anything I haven't seen before. It's just girl parts."

Dresser drawers slam open and shut hastily. "Yes, but they are my girl parts."

"Ah, and what beautiful girly parts they are," I tease.

I'm met with silence as she finishes putting on her clothes, and I feel almost insecure about my comment. I'm not lying about my assessment of her body; she really is truly gorgeous, but I've discovered that Carly is the type of girl who doesn't believe the good things about herself. Probably from too many years with that dickweed Jack. She's doesn't take a compliment well, and it's not because she doesn't appreciate them. It's that she doesn't know how to let them sink into her heart.

"Let's go, peeping Tom," she jokes as she smacks me in the chest with her pillow and steps into the hallway.

I grip onto the pillow and let out a small chuckle. I stand frozen in the doorway though. Feasting upon the delight of her ass in yoga pants as she trots down the hall to the kitchen, I just stand and enjoy the visual splendor.

Women always think smaller is better. I couldn't disagree more. I don't want to grab onto bones. I want meat, thick bubble butt muscle that can withstand a spanking now and again. Carly certainly has it, and now I find myself needing a minute to give my mini meat time to stand down.

"You coming?" she asks over her shoulder.

I snicker under my breath at her question and move the pillow to cover my lower half. "Um, be there in a minute," I say, clearing my throat.

Grandmas waxing lady parts, grandmas waxing lady parts, I think to myself. Finally, I take a deep breath, chuck the pillow back onto her bed, and run to catch up to Carly.

"Can we turn the music back on and dance some more," I say as I run past her and slap her delicious ass.

She startles and squeals. "You know that is sexual harassment, or something?"

"You bet your ass it is," I slyly say with a wink as I backpedal into the kitchen.

She shakes her head at my childish behavior, and I can't help but laugh. This woman is my friend, albeit a status I would love to elevate, but a friend at the moment nonetheless. I can only imagine the weight of the stress in her life right now; how she's not cracking from the pressure is beyond me. So any little comic relief I can provide, I will gladly oblige.

"Holy crap, did you buy the entire restaurant?" she asks, looking around at the copious amounts of takeout boxes piled on top of her table. "As good as this smells, my hips will forever pay for it and they already can't take another hit."

I lightly grab her elbow and turn her toward me, pissed that she would insult herself the way she does. "First, I didn't know what you liked and I didn't want you to have to just settle on something. Second, if you wanted to eat every damn morsel in the restaurant, I would be absolutely okay with it. In fact, I would pass you the fucking fork. And third, your hips are perfect. You are perfect. So, please don't insult yourself in front of me; it only pisses me off."

Her eyes search mine, looking for any untruth in my speech. It's like she's daring me to take it all back and call her the horrible names she's apparently been called in the past.

She backs away from my grasp, pulls out a chair, and sits down at the table. "Well then, let's have dinner," she finally announces.

"Well, all right then," I say with a nod, following her lead and sitting next to her.

She opens the boxes and scoops out small portions of everything available. They are so small that there is more plate showing than not. I follow behind her and scoop out the same entrees and place bigger piles of what she's chosen on her plate.

"You had to know that wasn't going to fly," I explain when she frowns at me. "If we are going to clog up our arteries with unhealthy grease tonight, then we are going balls to the wall."

I fill my plate and shovel a forkful of Low Mein noodles into my mouth, letting the droppings hangs from my lips before I slurp them back in. "Now eat, woman," I add, pointing my fork at her.

She smiles, taking a large heaping forkful of food and shoves it into her mouth similar to how I just had. "Oh, my God," she mumbles closing her eyes with her mouth filled. "This tastes so good," she adds, covering her mouth and wiping her lips with a napkin.

"Told ya," I laugh. "So, how did the meeting go?" I inquire now that she's more comfortable with me and we are eating casually.

"You know, I never in a million years thought that fostering or even adopting through foster care would have been an option for me. After meeting Leah, though, I just can't let her age out of the system the way Campbell did."

"What do you mean?" I ask. Campbell is one badass chick, but I know very little of her past. She keeps it professional, which is fine by me. Besides, Casen handles most everything band related with her. Still, my interest heightened.

"She was close with a foster family that she lived with briefly growing up, but she never was adopted. When she turned eighteen, she aged out of the system. Sure, the state helped to set her up with some programs to get her started, but really, she was on her own," she explains, the pain and sadness for her friend showing across her face.

"She had no family. We girls and Brooks became her family, but you could tell she always felt like she was a burden, that the holiday invites were charity or pity invites, even though they were the furthest thing from it."

"So did you guys help pay for things like parents would?" I ask. It seems pretty mindboggling that Campbell would have just been unleashed upon the world like a tether in the wind. How that seems fair to do to a kid is unsettling.

She laughs. "You know, that is the one area that Campbell is very different from the typical kiddo in the system. Her parents died and the people who were supposed to care for her turned her over to the state. Well, she had a trust set up for her when she came of age. It was for her only, and it was a very large sum of money. Every few years, a little more is sent to her."

My fork stops midway between my plate and mouth. "Whoa! So Campbell is some rich sugar momma?" I ask, stunned.

Carly giggles and nods. "I guess you could say that."

"Converse and tattered jeans, rockabilly, Led Zeppelin listening, Campbell is, what, like a millionaire?" I clarify, still unable to eat.

"Yup, but no one else had access to the money, so no one wanted her. That's how she ended up in the system so long," she says before taking a drink of her water.

"That's fucked up," I spit out, pissed that people would put money before kids. If something ever happened to one of my sisters and I had to take care of my nieces and nephews, yeah, it would be difficult, but I sure as hell would do it. With or without a payday on the other end. You do it because it's kids.

"It is," she says softly. She then hesitates for a moment before continuing her story. "So, when she introduced me to Leah, it was like seeing a younger version of Campbell, minus the trust fund, of course. She is a great kid, and I can't help but want to provide a home for her."

I take a long look at her, examining her hopeful expression, letting her words wash over me before responding. "You know Leah is not Campbell," I finally tell her. "And you can't save every kid you meet."

Her head snaps up to meet my eyes, her brows pulling together in dissatisfaction. "I know that," she says defensively. "I just want to help. I want to do for a child, even if it's just one child, what no one did for Campbell. There isn't anything wrong with that."

"Your heart is in the right place. I just hope you know what you're getting into," I advise.

"It's kids, you never know what to expect," she laughs. "Anyways, I have signed up for the class that potential foster parents are required to take and they have scheduled the visit to approve my home; then it's just a waiting game. Eventually, I'll possibly be able to adopt her since all parental rights have already been severed."

"How long does this all take?" I ask, surprised at the hoops someone would have to jump through. I guess I always assumed it would be a relatively quick and painless process. A kid needs a home, someone is offering a good home, done deal in my book.

"As long as we don't hit any snags, anywhere from one to two years for everything to be done, but the initial placement for fostering can happen within a few months."

"What does the ex have to say about all of this?" I ask, taking another heaping bite.

She sets her fork on her plate and scrunches her face. "I don't really care what he thinks anymore," she murmurs slowly, staring down at what's left of her meal.

"Thank goodness for that," I pop off, pushing away from the table. "He stopped by here earlier, seems like a gem of a guy," I add sarcastically as I gather our plates and take them to the sink.

"What?" she screeches, her eyes wildly searching mine.

"Yeah, he wasn't very happy to see me here, so I made sure to send him on his way with something to remember me by. He' a complete tool, by the way."

"What did you do?" she inquires hesitantly.

"Don't worry about it. I just let him know the divorce is his loss and there are plenty of guys willing to take care of you in areas that he fell short." I wink at her, but she just rolls her eyes.

"Oh, geez, I'm going to hear about that one." She blows out a long exhale and roughly rubs the pads of her fingers across her forehead, her stress showing through. "I just want it to be over so we can all move on. He's being so mean. I don't know how much more of him I can take."

I lean against the counter and watch the waves of despair and tension radiate from this gorgeous woman. She is so caring, so loving, even fun, but here she sits with the weight of the world on her shoulders because of a man. It's a man's job to take that worry away, not create it.

Jack is a piece of shit for making her feel this way and I want more than anything to make that stress disappear.

I want to make her laugh. I want to be the reason for every smile, every happy tear, and content sigh. She deserves that whether she believes it or not.

I pick up the bag of Starbursts and toss it across the room to her. "Grab your shoes and jacket; I'm showing you a good time tonight."

"What about the movies?" she asks, fumbling the bag before finally tucking it in like a football.

"Fuck the movies, we need to get crazy."

Carly

"Putt-Putt golf? That's your idea of crazy?" I tease as we pull into the parking lot of Putter's Pride.

He slides the stick shift into park and looks at me with a confused expression. "Since when is mini golf not killer?" he asks. "I offered fun, and I fully intend on following through."

I laugh and shake my head as we both step out of the car and move to the entrance. "I have to admit, it's been a long time since I've done this and I'm not very good at it, but I'll give it a shot."

Royce grabs my hand and squeezes, but then halts in the middle of the parking lot.

"Wait, we're forgetting something," he says before racing to the car and back to my side again. "We can't leave the candy behind," he tells me, handing me the bag and taking my hand once again. I haven't held a man's hand, other than Jack's, in years. The foreign feeling causes me to pull away with uncertainty.

"Relax, Carly," he says, pulling me back into his grasp. "We are here to enjoy each other. I won't take anything from you that you won't already want to give me." He smiles reassuringly, his boyish charm setting my mind at ease.

He shakes my arm until I let out a smile. "Come on. It's on like Donkey Kong, little lady," he says, pulling me through the entrance.

We stop at the front counter and Royce dings the bell to alert the attendant of our arrival. We have to wait for someone to rent our clubs from, but no one answers. I step out onto the course to look around for someone, but the course is pretty deserted. Only a small group of college-aged girls on the far end. Royce gets severely impatient, bouncing his hand continuously on the bell.

I elbow him in the ribs and he bends over and groans pretending as though he's critically injured. "Oh, stop it. You're fine," I laugh as I nudge him.

"Hello? Anyone here?" I shout into the back employee area.

We are met with strangled moans and grunts, sounds of papers and boxes falling onto the ground, and then the unmistakable shrill of a woman enjoying herself.

"Oh, my God, people are doing it back there," I whisper, pointing to the back area of the building.

Royce perks up, all fake injuries magically healed, and rushes to the employee door where I'm standing.

He bursts into laughter. "Maybe that's part of the employee benefits package," he jokes.

"What do we do?" I ask, walking back around to the front of the counter. "Should we leave?"

Royce grabs score cards, golf balls, and clubs from behind the counter, and throws a twenty on the register. "Hell, no. We came here to golf. I'm pretty sure they could care less if we just helped ourselves. I think they would prefer this to us interrupting whatever they have going on back there," he adds with a smirk.

A loud strangled noise of a couple climaxing spills out from the doorway and I want nothing more than to get away from this uncomfortable situation. "I'll meet you out there," I say over my shoulder as I walk out of the clubhouse and onto the course. I can't get out of there fast enough, and Royce just chuckles at my discomfort with our predicament.

Just as I reach the first putting obstacle, my embarrassment level spikes to an all-time high. My eyes widen and I search for anything to look at other than what is in front of me, but I fail miserably. Walking out of the backdoor and onto the course are our sexcapade culprits. The middle-aged man is extremely large and looks as though he just got out of the shower. However, I know it's sweat and not water rolling down his cheeks and neck. He's tucking his collared shirt into his sweatpants and wiping his face off when he notices me.

I turn away from him as quickly as I can and act casual, hoping Royce will join me and we can start our game like we didn't just see, or rather hear, the most unprofessional and inappropriate thing ever.

Nope, Royce walks through the main entrance arm in arm with our woman of the hour. Her hair and makeup look as though they have been recently corrected and smoothed out. She has the tell-tale post-coital glow and she looks as though she couldn't care less that we just heard her scream out Mr. Putt-Putt's name.

I admit to myself that I'm slightly jealous of seeing her cougar paws all over Royce. He's not mine, but there is a voice in my head screaming, *Warning, back off woman. I claim that man for myself.* At the very least, I want her to unhand him and reattach herself to Captain Sweatpants.

"Look who I found," Royce drawls with a crooked smile. "Wanda here said we were more than welcome to grab whatever equipment we needed and go ahead and start our game."

She rubs her hand up and down his bicep and giggles. Actually giggles like an immature school girl. "Sorry I was indisposed when you all came in. I am just so embarrassed. Welcome to our little establishment. I sure hope you two enjoy yourselves."

Lies, lies I tell you. She's not sorry, nor is she embarrassed. She is feeling rather good and satisfied. My eyes zero in on her exploring hand and I quietly hate her. In fact, I want to hit her with my golf club. Royce notices my squinted eyes and grimaced expression and shoots a befuddled look back to me. When I attempt to correct my expression, he smiles at my dismay.

"Thank you for your help. I think we'll get started with our game," Royce tells her while politely taking her hand off his arm.

"Absolutely. Just holler if you need anything. Bob and I will be around," she offers before leaving to join him at the side entrance. I watch her as she walks to him and explains her meeting with us. They both then wave to us, which only makes the entire exchange even more uncomfortable. I quickly throw my hand up and down in a stiff pathetic-looking wave and turn back around to face Royce.

His arms are folded across his chest and his smile is plastered from ear to ear.

"Well, that was awkward," I immediately tell him.

"Mmm hmm," he enunciates slowly, unmoving.

"What? That was seriously ridiculous. I can't even believe we are going to stay." I move past him, ignoring his suspicious grin.

"You were jealous," he finally announces.

"I certainly was not!" I defend, snatching a club and ball away from him and preparing for the first obstacle. He may have a slight point. There were a few pangs of jealousy coursing through me when I saw sex-crazed Wanda fawning over him, but those feelings don't matter. I'm in the middle of a divorce and I'm trying to hold my life together. The last thing I need is a romantic distraction, especially one like Royce. He's the lead singer of a band, not exactly father material.

"Okay, whatever you say," he chuckles following behind me.

Taking a deep breath, I grip the rubber on the top of the golf club and focus on the little white ball on the green. I size up the hole at the end of the course on the other side of the windmill obstacle, my eyes bouncing back and forth from the ball to the hole.

Royce's arms snake around me and his tattooed hands cover mine. I feel his chest press against my back and his head dip into my neck. I'm startled and I freeze, unsure what to do.

"If by chance you were jealous, all you have to say is yes, Carly. I would never let you regret that decision," he whispers.

My heart feels like it's going to pound out of my chest, my breath catches, and I'm left completely speechless. My head is telling me to push him away and set boundaries, but my body rejects the notion.

He lightly kisses my cheek and then moves away as quickly as he appeared. I hear him open the bag of candy he brought with us and unwrap some Starbursts as I take my first swing. I watch as the little ball rolls down the course and stops nowhere near the hole. It smacks against the front of the windmill and bounces back down the course.

"You want a do-over?" he asks, struggling with a mouth full of Starbursts.

I spin around to him. "No. It's your turn; it's only fair."

He gives me a nod and digs into the candy bag, pulling out a few squares of goodness and places the bag on the ground. I move out of his way so he can take his stance at the start of the course, but he grabs my hand and places a pink wrapped candy in my palm.

"Dessert," he says with a smile before moving away from me.

He stretches his body in an over exaggerated fashion, reaching the club above his head and twisting his midsection back and forth. He carries on with this for several minutes until I finally can't help but laugh.

"Oh my goodness, shoot already," I giggle.

He bounces back and forth on the balls of his feet while stretching his neck. "You can't rush genius; I'm preparing my body for battle," he explains in jest.

I smile, throw my hands up in playful surrender, and back off the course. He finally drops his ball and slides up next to it, aiming at the hole at the end of the course. He pulls the club far in the air close to his head and brings it down to the ball, stopping before striking it. He continues this motion several times before finally allowing the club to hit the ball, sending it sailing onto the next set of obstacles and interrupting the game of the only other people at the establishment.

"Man, I was so close," he says defeated. I laugh, appreciating his boyish attempt to make me feel better about my abysmal athletic showing. "At least we have more candy," he adds, handing me another pink Starburst before throwing a yellow into his mouth.

I gather my golf ball, abandoning this obstacle and we walk to the nearby course to retrieve Royce's ball.

"Sorry about that, ladies," he tells them as the very attractive blonde slides his ball into his hand. "We were getting a little out of hand over there."

"It's no problem at all," she coos with a perky smile. Her two friends whisper together behind her, before pulling her arm toward them and whispering into her ear. Her eyes shoot back to us and then her smile brightens. I've been around the band enough times to know what that look means…Royce has been recognized.

"You're famous, right?" the girl asks. "You're the singer for Absolution."

Yup, there goes our night.

Royce looks to me for the green light to acknowledge his famous status. I'm not exactly excited about it, but I go ahead and give him an approving nod. After all, this will only take a few seconds and then we can get back to our game.

"My name is Royce. Are you ladies fans?" he asks with an appreciative smile.

The girls jump up and down and pat down their hair in an attempt to make themselves more attractive. "I knew it!" the leader exclaims. "Can we get a picture with you?"

She slides her finger across her phone a few times to open the camera on it and shoves it to me. "Thanks, we'll only steal your brother for a second," she tells me before turning to look adoringly at Royce. "Unless he would like us to steal him a little longer," she coos.

"He's not my brother, but sure. Squeeze together and I'll take the picture for you," I tell her, waving my hands around like I'm directing traffic to get them to stand together.

They squeeze in tight, and the gorgeous blonde kisses his cheek. I quickly snap the picture. "Got it, looks good," I say with fake enthusiasm, expecting her to back away from Royce. Instead, she keeps her arm wrapped in his and pulls him down to whisper something in his ear. He sneers and then looks to me, which only prompts a frown on my face. Her hand glides up and down his arms lovingly, but I fight the urge to march over to her and break her arm, opting instead to let the jealous emotions bubble under my skin.

"Um, thanks, but I'm going to have to pass. I already have plans for the evening," he says, pulling his arm from her gasp.

"If you change your mind," she begins to say before looking back to me and then lifting up on her toes to whisper in his ear again to finish her sentence.

He nods and she giggles, but I want to throw up right there on top of both of their shoes.

The college coed crew turns to walk back to their course, excitement mixed with every step. I can't help but grin. As jealous as I was and am, I remember what it was like to be young and invincible. Rewind ten years and those girls could have been me and the girls, with Jen serving as our blonde leader.

"Did you really think she was his sister?" I hear one of the girls ask.

The blonde laughs and shakes her head. "No, but I had no other explanation why someone like him would be with someone like her. Look at her, it's like she didn't even try."

My smile slowly dwindles. I look down at my yoga pants and tank top and run my fingers through my hair, which has fallen flat from the day's stress.

They're right.

Jack was right. Who would want me?

Why would someone like Royce, who can have his pick of women, and has taken advantage of that fact, ever choose someone like me? The most I could ever hope for with him is a friendship.

My throat constricts and burns as my revelation coils itself around my psyche. The tears threaten to spill over my lids, but I hold them back.

Royce moves in front of me, but I can't manage to lift my head to face him.

"I just want to go home," I murmur, my voice straining.

He places his fingers under my chin and lightly forces me to meet his eyes. "I'll take you anywhere you want to go, as long as I get to be with you."

A tear escapes and I hastily wipe it from my cheek. I nod, affirming I want to leave, but instead of leading me back to his car, he grabs my hand and turns it palm up between us.

He places a pink Starburst in my hand and closes my fingers around it.

"Don't ever let anyone treat you like a yellow Starburst, Carly. You're a pink. You'll always be pink to me."

"Really?" I ask hesitantly.

"More than you know," he says before delicately kissing my forehead.

"Besides, pink Starbursts are always better than pink tacos," he jokes with a slide glance as he pulls away.

A strangled laugh breaks free. "Thank you, Royce. I needed that." His ability to take the pressure off of a situation is something I've come to appreciate about Royce. Jen thinks he's childish and hates how he makes a joke of everything. In this moment though, there isn't anyone else I'd rather have with me.

"Wait a minute, wasn't that line from some viral twitter feed or something?" I ask.

His guilty eyes slowly move to mine and he chuckles. "I think the pink tacos give it a little something extra. I thought the words fit and was hoping you don't follow the women's inspiration quotes feed."

I laugh at the idea of him reading daily chick motivation. "You really are a mystery to me, Royce. If I find copies of Cosmopolitan or Elle magazine at your place, we may have to deepen this conversation," I joke.

"Hey! Cosmo has some great articles!" he defends. "And the chicks on the covers are hot!"

We both grin and he stretches out his arm for me to take. "Come on, pink, let's blow this Popsicle stand."

I wrap my arm through his and he leads me past the college girls and Wanda without a second glance or goodbye. His sole focus is getting me where I want to go, together. My heart may have pounded a little harder in his arms.

Carly

How he talked me into this, I'll never know.

That's not true. I know exactly why he was able to convince me to go. Other than the girls, Royce has become my closest friend, so when he asked me to go to his niece's birthday party with him, I couldn't help but say yes.

Jack has Olivia for the weekend, and now that I have Leah's room all ready for her, she'll be moving in next week. So really, this is not only just a free weekend, but may be my last free weekend for a while. Fall is starting to take hold of the year and the girl's activities, and of course Jen's wedding will consume our lives.

"You nervous or something?" Royce asks, pointing to my bouncing knee. I'm trying to be cool and collected about going to this family gathering, but in all honesty, I'm freaking out a bit. He has said very little about them. I know he has sisters...and that's it. I asked the other guys in the band and they didn't even know he had sisters. Apparently, he keeps his family life private. Still, I'd like to be prepared if I'm walking into the snake's den. If Royce's personality is any indication, I should ready myself for the Raiders of the Lost Arc snake lair.

"I'm good," I lie. "Just had too much coffee."

His knowing smile and shake of his head suggest he's not buying my line of crap. So, I do what any girl would–change the subject.

"This is a really nice neighborhood. Do all of your siblings in the area?"

His eyes brighten and an aura of pure love radiates from him. "Yeah, my older two live just a few miles from each other and my younger two are in Ft. Collins at CSU. They come home often though. Family dinners every Sunday, you know."

I simply listen and nod, envious of his close-knit family. I get along with my family well, but we are a small, quiet crew. I'm picturing Royce's family as a loud, almost overwhelming group, which makes me even more nervous but also excited.

We pull into the idyllic driveway lined with perfectly manicured bushes. The white picket fence and wrap-around porch are Leave It to Beaver overload, and I can barely hide my jealousy. When I was a little girl and I pictured what my adult life would look like, this was what I wanted. The house, the huge family with so many grandchildren I would call out ten incorrect names before landing on the right one, and the husband who I would hold hands and grow old with, is what I envisioned.

But that's not what I got dealt. My cards included lies, divorce, and loneliness.

I swallow down my sadness for a dream lost and put on the most convincing smile I can muster as Royce opens the car door and leads me up the pathway to the front door. He knocks on the large red door as he opens it.

"Becca! We're here," he shouts into the house.

We are immediately met by a very familiar brunette and my smile fades.

"Everyone is in the kitchen," Hannah says with a warm greeting.

I turn toward Royce and narrow my eyes at him. I realize we aren't together, but to invite me to a family gathering and also invite his whatever she is, is just sick and wrong. I never would have agreed if he had told me I would serve at the third wheel pity invite.

"It's so good to see you again, Carly," she says.

Turning back to her, I whip out my manners. "It's good to see you too. I had no idea you were going to be here."

"Yeah, me either, but Mom threw a fit when I said I was going to stay in Ft. Collins for the weekend. Royce told us all you were coming, so I cancelled plans with my boyfriend and drove down."

My head snaps back and forth between the two of them.

"But I thought…" I begin to say. "But you said…" I can't seem to make my brain function enough to make a complete sentence. Synapses are misfiring and all I can think is Blackhawk Down! Blackhawk Down!

"You're not his sleeping buddy?" I finally spit out. *Sleeping buddy? Did I just seriously ask his sister if he was her sleeping buddy? There is no amount of alcohol that will fix this massive blunder.*

Her nose wrinkles and she looks to Royce, "Ewwww."

"What's ewwww?" a pretty blonde says, walking into the room.

"Oh, you know, Royce never told Carly I was his sister, so all this time, she thought I was sleeping with him," she says disgustedly.

"Ewwww," the blonde says, followed by a boisterous laugh. "Royce, if this sweet woman ever agrees to date you, I suggest you buy a lottery ticket because after putting her through this, you would be the luckiest man on Earth if she said yes," she adds.

Royce attempts to defend himself, but his sisters shush him and Hannah speaks over him.

"I'm sorry, Carly," Hannah says. "I thought he told you."

"I'm Becca," the blonde introduces herself, holding out her hand. "Please don't let my brother's poor social skills sway your feelings about our family. I promise, most of us are normal." She pulls me into a hug and leads me into the kitchen where the rest of the family is.

There are smiling people completely filling the space. "Everyone, this is Carly," Becca says when we enter the kitchen. She is still holding onto my shoulder, and Royce doesn't try to pull me away. Instead, he follows close behind and allows his sister to run the show.

I offer a wave similar to the wave that Hannah once gave me and the girls. "Great to meet everyone," I shyly say.

An older woman with shoulder-length silver hair moves around the kitchen island and briskly walks to me. As she gets closer, I can see where Royce and his sisters get their looks. She pulls me into a warm embrace and solidly wraps her arms around me.

"We've heard so many great things about you, hun. I'm glad my son finally got the guts to bring you around. You're actually the first girl he's ever brought home."

My eyes widen and find Royce in the sea of people. He looks as uncomfortable as I feel. He swoops in and pulls me away from his mother.

"All right, womenfolk. That's enough fawning; you're going to scare her off," he says, wrapping a tattooed arm around me. His mother smiles at his affectionate gesture. I feel like I've just been through some kind of auditioning process and I've moved onto the call back list. I just don't know what I was interviewing for.

Royce

Carly spent the evening wiggling her way into my family's hearts just as she has mine. She laughed with my sisters, listened to every embarrassing story my mom and dad shared, sang happy birthday for my niece, and even played a game of checkers with the kids. I knew they would love her, but I needed their green light before I pursued anything. My family means everything to me, so the girl I decide to date needs to mesh with everyone, and Carly meshes.

My mom wasn't lying when she said I've never brought a girl home. I've never had a girlfriend to bring home. Have I slept with women? Fuck, I'm surprised my dick hasn't fallen off. Have I actually dated any of them, or introduced them to my parents? Hell no.

Carly is different. She is settle down, wife and kids, growing old together different, and I'm willing to wait however long it takes to have the chance to be her different, her something special.

My mother's words play over and over in my head as we walk back to the car after the party. 'She's a sweetheart, Royce. Don't break her heart.' Her words repeat in my head and are so damn true; I'm scared to death. I'll do anything in my power not to hurt this woman. I just don't know if she'll give me the chance to prove it.

My shoes pound against the pavement and with each step I wish more and more that my sister had a longer driveway. We reach the car quicker than my courage can materialize, and when she reaches out for her door handle, it takes me a moment to realize it's now or never.

"Wait, I have something for you," I tell her, hitting the key remote to open the trunk.

She retracts her hand and stands surprised as I walk to the back of the car and pull out a large wrapped present.

"I think I've had enough surprises for one night," she says with a giggle.

"I'm hoping you might actually want this one, though," I say, handing her the gift. The box is huge; I could barely fit it in the trunk, and she has to set it on the cement to open it.

She looks at me suspiciously and I have to urge her to tear open the wrapping paper. When the flaps of the box open and reveal the hundreds of Ping-Pong balls inside, her brows pull together in confusion.

"There's a card," I explain before she can ask.

Reaching into the box, her hands maneuver around the little white balls trying to find the card. I want to laugh, but my nerves stifle the notion. She finally finds the envelope and rips it open, pulling out the card inside.

"I finally found the balls to ask you out," she reads aloud.

Her silence has me freaking the fuck out. I was hoping to score points for creativity, but I'm thinking my move ended up immature. Just as I open my mouth to explain, grovel, apologize, take your pick, she burst into laughter.

She laughs so hard tears pour down her cheeks, and I'm speechless. I don't know if I've insulted her, if I blew my chance, but I'm thinking I'm in danger of being slapped.

She dries her eyes with the back of her jacket sleeve and takes a deep breath. She doesn't say yes, she doesn't say no, she says nothing at all. No, Carly steps forward, moves up onto her tip-toes, and kisses me.

I'm shocked at first, but then I take over, deepening a kiss that I've waited weeks to relive. When my lips touch hers, I taste a future I never thought I would have, and with every passing second I become more and more addicted to a love I could never let go of.

Carly

The mountain of paperwork in the backseat is staggeringly overwhelming. When my lawyer called today and asked me to pick it all up and go through it, I was expecting a few folders, not an entire box. The accountant hired to audit our accounts for the divorce case found things that needed explaining, so instead of the date Royce and I had planned for the evening, here I am, going through it all.

"Label and identify all accounts and transactions that you're familiar with," is what the accountant said. The task is daunting, since I never really concerned myself with our financials. Jack always took care of everything; he is an investment banker after all. I'm not sure what help I would be with all of this.

Thankfully, Vivian and Brooks are keeping Olivia to work on their group Halloween costumes and Leah is staying the night at a friend's house so I can spend the evening trudging through the numbers.

I hoist my purse over my shoulder and open the backseat to load the cardboard box into my arms; I'm shocked by the weight. Never in a million years would I have thought we would have money in so many places and accounts and real estate ventures with my name on them. Joint savings and checking accounts and life insurance policies were all I was aware of.

Apparently, Jack was keeping more than just a vasectomy from me.

My phone dings just as I reach the steps to the house. I struggle to quickly unlock the door and get inside. I nearly drop the box and its contents on the ground before I can get it deposited onto my kitchen table. Digging through my purse on my way to my bedroom, I finally find my phone and the text message waiting for me.

> Royce: *Are you sure you don't want me to come help, maybe just keep you company?*

I pause in the hallway to think about my answer. Would I like him to come over? Yes. Should he come over? No. I'm about to dive into a swimming pool of lies, and I don't want to depend on him as my life preserver. I need to face this mess, this sham of a marriage on my own, and it might be a very emotional experience. I don't want him here to see that, to see me like that.

> Me: *Thank you for offering, but I need to do this alone.*

I shoot off the text and walk into my bedroom. Flipping on the light, I notice the light is on in the master bathroom. Leah must have forgotten to shut it off before she left for her friend's house. I turn it off and head to my armoire in my closet to hang up my scarf and put away my jewelry from the day when my phone dings again.

> Royce: *I'm booorrrred.*

I laugh, thinking about him rolling his eyes and giving his best pretend whine, like Olivia would. I slip off my shoes and kick them to the back of the closet as I type my response.

> Me: *I'm sure the boys are up to something. Give them a holler.*

I'm rummaging through my pajama draw when my phone buzzes again.

> Royce: *Shitty alternative. I may or may not show up on your doorstep. Skip the sweatpants and wear something pretty for me. Love ya, pink.*

Now it's my turn to roll my eyes, but I can't help but smile. Deciding to play it safe, I select the yoga pants instead of the cozy flannel set I had planned on wearing. The silly smile on my face is still in place as I lift my eyes from the drawer of clothes to the mirror attached to the dresser.

I'm shocked by what I see.

Jack.

When my eyes meet his, my smile disappears and is quickly replaced with fear.

I drop the clothes and try to punch the buttons on the phone. Before I can scream, before I can run, he hits me across the back of the head with something hard and unforgiving. I feel the blood drip from the wound as I fall to the floor.

I fight to remain conscious, but the darkness is too much and I drowned in the softness of its embrace. A black abyss surrounds me and my mind tumbles away from the reality of the moment. I hear his footsteps and see his hand pick up my phone before the blackness takes me.

The throbbing in my head is provoking waves of nausea like I have never known. I try to cover my mouth, but my hands are frozen, stuck in place. I struggle against the ropes which bind my hands behind the chair I'm sitting in, but it's futile. They are tight, and every time I move, they bite my skin even more. My head is down and shoulders are slouched, but I try to take in my surroundings. I slowly crack open my eyes but the light forces them shut again and exacerbates the pain in my head.

I hear a defeated moan escape my lips followed by footsteps. His boots against the tile cause me to freeze, pretend like I'm still unconscious.

"No need to pretend, Carly," Jack whispers next to my ear. "I know you're awake. Besides, our other guest will be here soon, and you won't want to miss it."

"Why are you doing this?" I ask hesitantly as I work to open my eyes.

"Why?" he huffs, pacing in front of me. I can feel the anger rolling off him and it terrifies me.

"Please, Jack. Let me go. I haven't done anything to you," I plead, my voice trembling from the tears I'm holding at bay and the knot in my throat.

"You took everything from me, you stupid bitch!" he roars as his hand flies back and swings forward connecting with the side of my face. My head snaps to one side and a light flashes behind my eyelids. The violent impact makes my head pound and the nausea to spike, causing bile to rise in my throat.

The skin on my cheek tingles and the taste of iron fills my mouth. The crushing pain forces a sob from my chest.

"What do you want?" I cry, tears now streaming down my face.

"You know, I almost feel sorry for you. You've always been a little slow on the uptake, but your stupidity astounds me at times," he heckles as he pulls out a chair from the kitchen table, flips it around, and takes a seat next to me.

"Our marriage was one of convenience. I needed your identity to embezzle the money I was stealing from my clients. A few more years and I would have had the nest egg I wanted. But then you had to go and get nosey and fuck up my whole plan."

"What are you talking about? We have a daughter together."

"The kid? Yeah, that was one big damn misstep," he says, cutting me off. "I made sure to correct that mistake from happening again."

He taps the box from my lawyer's office that's on the table. "I was planning to slowly start siphoning funds from the accounts and businesses that you are CEO of, to new off-shore accounts. I just needed to disappear, and if anyone had questions, you would be the one to have to answer for them as your name was all over the documentation. That was the plan, but now Plan B will have to work."

"Did you really think you could get away with something like that?" I ask, bewildered by what I am hearing.

"Everything was working well, until that bitch Campbell got involved and encouraged you to hire a lawyer. That audit has ruined everything. Thankfully, my name isn't anywhere near that box of fraud; it's all on you, babe. Everyone will see me as the unsuspecting widower whose wife was caught up in illegal activities on the verge of getting caught. I'll just dump the brat in some boarding school, and start over with what money I've managed to move already and the nice little life insurance policy you've left for me."

"You can't do this," I cry, fighting against the ropes.

"Oh, Carly," he says sarcastically. "I already have. As soon as our other loose end gets here, I can finish this up and be done with you."

The doorbell rings, and Jack covers my mouth as I try to scream for Campbell to run, to get help.

"We don't need you ruining the surprise," he says as he replaces his hand with a piece of duct tape. He then pushes the chair I'm sitting in away from the table and closer to the corner of the kitchen. Jack picks up my cell phone and sends a text message before winking at me and leaving the kitchen.

"Carly? I'm here," I hear Campbell shout from the entrance. "Where are you and what is so important that I had to drop everything and get here right now?"

I pull and tug against the rope, but I accomplish nothing but irritating the skin further. My wrists feel raw, every movement sending stinging sensations up my forearms.

"Carly? Where are you?" she calls, her footsteps getting closer to the kitchen. As soon as I see her in the kitchen doorway, I try to scream but the tape makes my voice sound more like just muffled noise. Her eyes widen in shock and she rushes to me to rip the tape from my mouth. I pull away from her as the tape tears tiny hairs from my skin and my eyes water.

"Jack," I pant. "He's in the house and planning to kill us both. You have to run, Campbell, get help."

"What?' she exclaims as she runs around to untie my hands. "What is this all about? Why would he want to hurt you? He's the one who was cheating."

As soon she frees my hands, the ease in tension forces my shoulders to heave forward. A warm ache radiates from my muscles. She hustles back around to help me from the chair before pulling her cell phone from her pocket.

"You don't understand," I insist, grabbing the box from the table. "We need to get out of here. We can call the police once we're in your car."

"You really should have listened to her," I hear Jack say as he reenters the kitchen. "Now there's nowhere to run." I spin around, tightly grasping the box in both hands. Jack is standing behind Campbell with his knife held to her throat. She is breathing hard, her neck grazing the blade with every exhale.

"Put the box back, and use that duct tape to bind her wrists," he demands.

I hesitate, unsure of what would be the best way to help my friend. Do I run and get help, trusting that he doesn't hurt her, or do I comply with the hope she and I can get ourselves out of this mess together?

"Now," he yells, digging the knife into her neck, just enough to draw blood.

"Okay. Okay, Jack. Please don't hurt her," I plead, placing the cardboard box down and grabbing the duct tape.

I slowly spread the tape around her wrists, but my eyes never leave hers. "Don't," she mouths as I layer the tape.

I tear off the piece from the roll and grip it firmly. "I can't leave you here," I say quietly.

Jack throws Campbell to the ground and grabs me to tape my hands together, just like Campbell's. "You have a chance to get away and you waste it? You are as stupid as I always thought," he huffs, winding the tape around my wrists and tearing the end from the roll." He pushes me to the ground next to Cam and pops the lid off of the box.

Sliding the chair in front of us and taking a seat, he picks through the papers from the box. "No one had to die, you know," he explains. "I just wanted the money, and then I was going to disappear. But then you two complicated everything. There's no way around it now, you two can't exist."

"And how do you expect to keep your name away from our deaths?" Campbell pops off. There is no fear in her voice, no hesitation, just a sass I've never heard from her before. "I've always thought you to be a fairly intelligent man, Jack, but you're delusional if you think you'll walk away from this."

Jack just laughs as he scatters some of the papers across the table. "You're right, Campbell. The difficulty is going to be staging it just right. The murder suicide needs to look perfect. But you know what?" he says, tucking the knife into the waist of his jeans and smiling at her.

We both shake our head.

"If all else fails, it's nothing a little house fire can't cover up." He doesn't give us a second thought as he turns toward the kitchen cabinets and begins opening drawers, looking for a lighter.

Fear completely takes hold of my senses while Cam's confidence doesn't waver. She is calm and collected, like she has a plan she just hasn't filled me in on.

They say when you have nothing to lose, you're not afraid of losing. Sitting here, looking at Campbell, I've never believed that more. She has no family, no husband, and no children. It's just her and she's willing to look death in the face and spit on him, while I sit here frozen in place with everything to lose. My girls need me. I can't let them be sent away to boarding school or another foster family or group home, yet here I sit…terrified.

I think the saying is wrong; it's the fighters like her that always survive.

Campbell nods toward Jack who is searching through the papers in the box and then quietly slides up the wall. She gathers her bound hands above her head and then quickly forces them down upon her thighs, causing the tape to tear. A grunt escapes her lips and Jack turns to see her pulling the rest of the tape apart and away from her wrists.

He reaches for his knife as both of them lunge for each other in the middle of the kitchen. Panicked, I stand and attempt to remove the tape the same way Cam did, but it won't separate. I frantically pull and tug, but they are stuck together.

Jack throws her against the refrigerator and she struggles against the arm holding the knife. The thud of her back hitting the stainless steel grabs my attention. She can't hold him off much longer without help.

As fast as I can, I charge toward them and jump onto Jack's back, pulling his hair and scratching his face. The three of us crash against the fridge and Campbell lets out a scream. When Jack pulls away from her, she slinks to the floor. I'm entirely focused on Jack, clawing, biting, trying everything I can to hurt him. But he then gains his footing, spins, and flips me over his back onto the table.

The box flies off and documents fill the air. A shooting pain splinters through my back, and it knocks the wind out of me.

Coughing, I fall off the table onto the floor where I'm met with Jack's boots; the steel-toe connects with my rib. The crack followed by the inability to draw a full breath tells me it's broken. I roll away from him, trying to get away, protect myself as much as possible from any further assault.

"I don't know where you think you're going," he says, grabbing my hair and forcing me to my feet. Once standing, I see Campbell on the floor, unconscious, with a pool of blood surrounding her.

Tears fill my eyes as I realize I'm on my own.

If I want to live, I have to save myself.

Everything hurts. I'm so battered, but if I don't act, it won't matter.

"I thought I would do this quick, show a little mercy. Not anymore, Car. You're going to feel every bit of this night," he rasps, tugging my hair back.

I try to think as quickly as I can. I'm at such a disadvantage, my hands are still bound, I'm injured, and he's bigger. There's no way I can fight my way out this. I have to get out of his grasp and run. I have to get help here for Campbell.

Jack is keeping me close to his chest, one hand in my hair and the other clutching the knife. He's moving us backward across the kitchen, as to keep an eye on Campbell.

I mentally prepare myself to get away. Just before we reach the entry to the kitchen, I bring my foot down to stomp on his instep.

"What the fuck?" he exclaims, stumbling back. I lace my fingers together and rear my elbow back, landing it in his stomach, knocking him further off balance. He lets go of my hair, but then trips over the box, which had flown off the table.

I turn to run, but he grabs my shirt and pulls me down with him as he falls to the floor. We land and the metal of the knife scrapes across the hardwood floor.

It's my chance. Possibly my last chance.

Kicking my legs at him as hard as I can to get out of his reach, he finally unhands me and I'm able to roll away from him. I scramble, my elbows and knees pounding on the hardwood with each movement, but my mind blocks the pain, and I stay concentrated on the objective.

Get the knife and run.

Get the knife and run.

He's crawling, stumbling behind me, my moment of freedom slipping away. His groans and profanities are getting closer, but my panic subsides as adrenaline takes over. I feel the cool metal of the knife in my shaking hands, and I grip it tightly, letting its slick body meld to my skin. It provides a moment of peace, security in a time of chaos.

Jack grabs my shoulder to force me to my feet, and as I turn, I jab the blade forward. I put every bit of my might, every ounce of energy I have left, into holding that knife.

His body strains as the blade enters his chest and I hold my breath, waiting for whatever absolution will follow. He inhales deeply as though it will be his last, but I hang onto the blade, I cannot will myself to let go.

"I won't let you win," I scream, tears flowing down my cheeks.

He exhales and his body crumples on top of me, crushing me below him. I feel the life drain out of him, and it's only when he stops breathing that I find the will to breathe again.

My heart is pounding; my breathing is to point of hyperventilating.

Jack is dead.

I've killed him; his motionless body on top of me a reminder of that.

I gain some semblance of my composure and push him off me, the knife still solidly buried in his chest.

"Oh, my God," I hear Royce stammer. I look up to see him standing in the living room taking in the bloody scene.

"Please, call the police," I choke out.

He rushes to me and breaks the tape from my wrists. "What the fuck happened here?" he asks, examining me for injuries.

"I'm okay. This isn't my blood. Please just call the police."

He nods and pulls his cell phone from his pocket. He wraps an arm around me and steers me from the living room, but I break away.

"No. Campbell," I say adamantly before turning from him and rushing to the kitchen.

I see her where I left her, propped against the refrigerator and I can't get to her fast enough. I kneel down next to her and try to shake her awake, but she isn't moving. Blood has saturated her shirt where the blade penetrated her abdomen.

I grab a towel from the drawer next to us and press it against her wound to stop the bleeding. Resting my head on her chest, I listen for a breath, a heartbeat, anything that would tell me she's going to be okay.

"Please don't go, Campbell," I whisper to her. "You're my family."

Lakin

I don't know what prompted me to get in my car, something just felt off. Carly is never intrusive or insistent, but her texts were. She was adamant that Campbell come over immediately, and that's not like her. Something is wrong.

I was tense when Campbell left for Carly's house, but when Campbell wouldn't return any of my texts, and then Carly ignored me as well, I began to worry. Then when a text came in from Royce to get to Carly's house, I grabbed my keys and headed in the direction of the girls as quickly as I could.

He wouldn't tell me what happened, just that I needed to get there, which only made my fear intensify. I don't even know how long it took to get there; it was like my car floated there. My mind was not focused on the road; my thoughts were devoted only to Campbell.

When I pull onto the street, the red and blue lights that illuminate the sky only confirm my worry.

All I can think is that Cam needs me.

The emergency lights bounce off house windows, blinding me as I park and jump out of my car. There are so many cars and emergency personnel everywhere, I have to leave my car several hundred yards from the house.

I race down the sidewalk, sending a little prayer with each step that I will find her all right when I reach the house. I go unnoticed by police until I reach the taped off driveway. I duck under the yellow rope and am immediately met by armed officers.

"Sir, you need to stay behind the tape; this is a crime scene," the man says matter-of-factly, placing a hand on my chest to stop me.

"No, I need to get in there," I insist.

"Sorry, we are investigating a major incident that occurred here tonight. If you have any information that might be helpful to the case, we have detectives who would like to speak with you, but if not, we need you to stay behind the perimeter.

My stomach drops when I hear him describe the evening as an incident that would require detectives; it means that my entire world may have just been turned upside-down. The possibility that I might have lost Campbell barrels me over and brings tears to my eyes.

"The coroner is ready to move the body," an officer announces out the front door to a group of officers in the driveway. "Can we get a path cleared for the van?"

My mind becomes dizzy with the possibility of unbearable grief and I struggle to swallow down the knot in my throat.

Unable to stand there any longer, I rush past the officer and push my way through the other emergency workers. I make it all the way to the front door before a swarm of hands restrain me.

"Get off me!" I shout. "My wife is in there!" I rage against their grip, but make little progress.

"Sir, you need to calm down. Who is your wife?" one of the officers asks.

"Campbell Ryan, where is she? Is she okay?" I ask frantically, straightening my clothes once they release me.

"The women were transported to the hospital. One was in critical condition when we got here. Paramedics had to do CPR upon arrival. I haven't heard their current status though," a detective explains. "Let me get some information for you and I can have an officer escort you to the hospital."

I exhale as I bend at the waist and rest my hands on my knees to gain my bearings. "I need to get to her. Just tell me which hospital," I murmur, trying to catch my breath.

I called Jen and Vivian on the way to hospital. They bombarded me with questions, but I had no answers for them. All I could offer was a location. I tried calling Royce's phone, but it continually went straight to voicemail. As soon as I find a parking spot, I storm through the emergency room doors.

Brooks, Vivian, Casen, and Jen arrive just after I do, and together we flood the nurse's station to inquire about Campbell and Carly.

"We need information about two women who were brought here," Vivian says.

"What are their names and what is your relationship to the patients?" the nurse asks.

"Our friends--"

"My wife," I say, speaking over the group.

Everyone's mouths drop open as they slowly turn in disbelief to stare at me.

"Campbell Ryan, she is my wife," I clarify. "Please tell me where I can find her."

"Let me just go check if she has been moved yet," the nurse nods and disappears down the long emergency room hallway.

"Excuse me? You two are married? As in justice of the peace, for all eternity, make a million babies, married?" Jen rambles.

When I don't say anything, Brooks intervenes on my behalf. "He only said that so we could get information," he tells them. "They won't release anything to anyone but family. Right?" He looks to me to confirm my lie, but I still say nothing which is met with a deep brotherly dissatisfied expression.

"You guys! About fucking time!" Royce shouts from down the hallway, gaining the attention of many of the emergency personnel. However, I find his interruption to be greatly appreciated. He waves us toward him, encouraging us to follow him.

The women rush past me, unfazed by the earlier topic of marriage, but Brooks hangs back.

"This conversation isn't over, little brother," he whispers to me before taking a step to follow his wife and the others. The disappointment in his tone isn't caused by the fact I'm married to Campbell, but that I kept it a secret from him. I get it, I really do, but I could give two fucks right now. My sole concern is for her and no one else.

"It's done, Brooks. We've been married since Vegas," I tell him, causing him to halt his stride. "Campbell wanted to wait until after Jen's wedding to say anything, but it is what it is. I love her and we are married; get over it." I try not to insert any prick attitude into my delivery, but with the stress of the situation, I know I've failed miserably.

Brooks shakes his head and carefully examines me. After a long pause, he outstretches his hand. "Well, I guess this is congratulations then."

A hint of a small smile breaks through my cold expression, my fear and apprehension, easing. I say nothing, though; I just shake his hand.

"Now, let's go make sure your girl is okay," he says, wrapping an arm around me as we walk down the hall. "By the way, I'm not getting you a wedding present," he jokes.

Together we enter the room that Royce leads us to; everyone cramped along the walls around Carly, who's in the hospital bed. Every piece of skin that is uncovered is black and blue; she is completely tattered. Her makeup has smeared down her face from the tears she's shed. But other than the bruises, she thankfully appears okay.

I search each of the faces, expecting to see Campbell up against the wall with the others, but she's not here.

"Where is she?" I ask breathlessly.

Her eyes bounce down to her blankets, unable to look at me.

"I'm glad you're okay, Carly, but where is Campbell?" I say sternly.

My tempter flares, knowing she is in a hospital room as well, but instead of having her friends and her husband there to comfort her, she's alone. "Why in the hell is she alone? How dare you all leave her, and expect me to abandon her as well. Where in the fuck is my wife?" I shout.

Royce walks over and places his hand on my shoulder, attempting to calm my roar. I can hear my heartbeat trying to pound out of my chest. My entire body feels like it's shaking from the anxiety of the moment.

"They're working on her, Lakin," he says hesitantly.

"What do you mean?" I can barely get the words out through the constriction in my throat.

"She has several smaller defensive knife wounds that are easily repairable with sutures, but somehow in the fight she was stabbed badly in the abdomen. She was bleeding internally, so they couldn't be sure of the damage until they got her into the operating room. She lost a lot of blood, Lakin."

I stand motionless, stunned by the news of her status. My heart just ripped into a million tiny pieces and I have no control over whether or not it will be mended. I feel everyone's eyes on me, staring but unable to say anything. The unease and grief of the situation is palpable.

Royce clears his throat to break the unyielding silence. "They gave me her things; the nurse said she couldn't wear jewelry in the operating room," he says, reaching into his pocket and pulling out her necklace.

He holds it up, allowing her flower and love token to dangle from his fingers. The sight of it is almost unbearable. She never takes it off, and here she is in her most vulnerable state, without it, without me.

I take a deep breath and then wrap my hand around the cool metal. "Nabac dom gan, mo ghrá," I murmur, as I rub my thumb across the engraving that is now stained with dried blood.

"Forget me not, my love," I repeat with more conviction, before turning and leaving the room. I walk through the doors, leaving my grief behind in search of whatever hope I can find.

Fall 2015

Campbell

I walk through the doors of *A Scone's Throw* and fight my way back to our table, but I'm met with stunned faces and Carly's tears. I wasn't going to miss this day for anything, but apparently the girls thought differently.

I pull out my usual chair and take a seat at our table. "Did you really think I wouldn't be here for this?" I ask them.

"Well, yeah," Carly chokes out. "You are supposed to be on that European tour. There were no open days in the schedule. How is this even possible?" she asks.

The waitress comes over and places a water on the table in front of me and I thank her with a smile. "Some things came up, including this, so I took a few days off and flew home," I explain.

"Since when is it that easy?" Jen counters. "I've been on a tour, remember? They suck balls and there is no 'I'm taking a few days off.'" She scowls at me, daring me to show my hand. I know she's right; there is no time off during tour. It's all or nothing.

"I would rather not talk about it just yet. Today is Carly's day," I try to deflect. I've known Jen long enough to know she won't settle for that explanation, so I packed my purse with souvenirs in preparation for sharing my secret, just in case I'm forced to.

"We are a family, Campbell," Carly says. "This isn't my day; this is a special day for all of us." Her smile beams and it makes me so thankful I was able to be here for this. I've actually been in town for a few days, but I wasn't ready to see them all just yet. Lakin and I needed to get our own situation handled before explaining everything to them.

"Did you quit? Did the tour end early? How is this even possible," Vivian asks as she takes a drink of her coffee and places it back on the table.

I wiggle in my chair and take a long pull of my ice water; I'm a little uncomfortable with the direction of the questions. I don't really want this day to be about me; we should be focusing on Carly.

"I've decided to quit for now," I say quickly. When stunned looks bounce back at me, I continue with my vague explanation. "Lakin and I have other things we need to focus our attention on. As much as I love the job, I'm going to take some time away."

I'm immediately bombarded with a million questions from every direction.

"Is there something wrong that we should know about?" Vivian asks.

"I thought everything had healed from the surgery?" Jen says, panicked. "You need to tell us right now, what in the hell is going on."

"Music is your life; you can't quit. What happened?" Carly demands, her smile fading and replaced with a look of concern.

I had a feeling this would happen, which is why I brought presents. Knowing I can't backtrack and rewind this conversation, I resign myself to divulge the information I have been hiding from them.

"I've been back for a few days," I exhale. "Lakin and I went to the doctor a few days ago, but we weren't prepared for the news we got. I planned to tell you, but we needed a few days to process everything."

"Holy canola oil, you need to just say it," Carly interrupts. "This has been the most difficult year of our lives, trying to move past everything that Jack did to us. I can't bear to think about possibly losing you, so if you are sick or hurt, you need to just tell us."

I nod without a smile and reach into my bag for the presents within it and pull out the silver-wrapped gifts.

"Oh fuck, she came with gifts; this is really bad," Jen blurts out, fanning herself like she's trying to hold tears in.

Vivian and Carly wrap their hands and arms around each other as I push the gifts in front of them. Their eyes zero in on the packages, but they don't move their hands to open them. Jen instantly pushes her gift back to me.

"I can't. I love gifts, but not like this. Take it away," she insists.

I laugh at all of them and push the package back in front of her. "Just open them," I tell them reassuringly.

They each hesitantly open their gifts and uncover the jewelry box inside. One by one, they pop open the top of the box and I'm met with three very different expressions. Vivian exhales loudly, Jen scowls, but Carly looks up at me with tears staining her cheeks.

"I don't get it," Jen announces befuddled, lifting the silver charmed bracelet from its box. "How is this a clue about what's going on with you?"

I had each specially designed for them with a flower and a quote inscribed on the heart-shaped charm. Vivian's with a clover, Jen's with a dandelion, and Carly's with a forget-me-not. She obviously didn't look at the entire bracelet.

"Read the back," Vivian whispers forcefully in her direction.

She flips it over and slowly reads the back to everyone at the table. "The only thing better than having you as a sister, is my children having you as their aunt." Her eyes immediately bounce to mine.

"But I thought..." Jen tappers off, pausing for a moment before continuing. "The damage from the attack would make it difficult if not impossible to have children?"

I grab Carly's trembling hand and snap the bracelet around her wrist. "Apparently not impossible after all," I say, smiling at her. "The babies are due next spring."

Shocked, Jen spits out her coffee across the table and I dodge the path of the spray. "Babies, as in plural?" Jen asking, not even bothering to clean up her mess on the table. "You're having twins?"

I giggle at her reaction and simply nod.

Carly gradually stands and pulls me up from my chair to stand with her. Her arms wrap around me and squeeze me tightly.

"I've always been told you can't choose your family," she whispers in my ear. "They say you should hold them dear, because at times, your family will be all that you have."

She pulls away and squares her shoulders at me with every bit of confidence she can pull together, a confidence I don't think I've ever seen. "Those people are wrong; the four of us have created a family together, all of us. I hold you dear not because I have to but because I want to and I'd sacrifice all I have to protect that family."

Jen and Vivian stand and circle their arms around us creating a group hug in the back section of the coffee house, a place that has been a staple over the last few years. We momentarily bask in one another's comforting embrace.

I back away with a smile and grab my purse, slinging it over my shoulder. "Now, let's go add one more to this crazy family of ours."

The amount of people who walk through the courthouse doors is impressive; we look more like a mob ready for a rock show rather than witnesses at an adoption proceeding. Everyone is dressed in their very best and is lugging presents for Leah to officially welcome her into our little group.

After the incident, I wasn't convinced this day would happen. Leah was removed from Carly's home that night and placed in a group home. She then wasn't allowed back until the Department of Child Services could assess the safety of the situation and placement. Those months were extremely difficult for all of them. There were times that I thought they wouldn't be able to weather the storm and would collapse under the strain of their grief.

Chatter and laughter fill the room, and the vibration of everyone's joy for the moment is seen on every face I see, except one…Leah's. I watch as each member of our little gang takes turns saying things to her and pulling her into a big hug, but each time she meets them with an uncomfortable smile.

Her long blonde hair falls in front of her face to hide her anxious expression, but I see it, I see her.

When Royce pulls Carly away from the group and Leah is left alone, I take my opportunity to talk with her, to tell her all of the things I wish Sharon had told me decades ago.

She is sitting on the bench, her neatly pressed floral dress fits her perfectly, but she is obviously uncomfortable in it. I'm not surprised; dresses have probably never been in her wardrobe before Carly came into her life. I learned early that jeans and a hoodie were the route to go when you have a very limited amount of clothing. It makes it less obvious to your classmates that you have nothing, that you wear the same clothes every day. She no doubt has learned the same lesson.

"You look very nice today, Leah," I compliment as I take a seat on the bench next to her.

"I'm not good with dresses," she says as she pulls at the shoulder strap of the dress and then flattens the fabric across her knees. "I'm used to pants," she adds in a whisper, a sense of shame rolling off her.

I sigh loudly, knowing all too well the feelings she's experiencing. "Me too, remember?" I tell her with a smile and a slight nudge with my knee. Her eyes meet mine, begging for reassurance.

"You know I never got this far," I tell her. "I grew very close with one of my foster parents and I thought maybe I would be adopted, but it just didn't happen. I wished and wished to be in the seat you're sitting in now."

"I know. I'm very thankful, excited even, but I'm so nervous," she explains, her hands wrestling with each other with anxiety. "When I was in different placements or group homes, I just existed. I flew under the radar and stayed out of trouble, but there was never any pressure to be or do more than just survive."

She looks down at her dress again and fluffs the cloth. "That's different now. I want this, I really do it's just..." she pauses and looks around for any listening ears before continuing. "The world I knew is ending and I don't know if I'll be any good at living in my new world."

I nod and reach into my bag for the final gift I had prepared for today. I place the little box in her lap, and direct her to open it. As she carefully tears away the wrapping I begin my explanation of the gift, hoping she finds some comfort in my words.

"When I was in the system, my life was a series of landings. I never knew where I would be landing next, and I was both hopeful and nervous about the idea of possibly finding a permanent home. What if I didn't live up to their expectations? Adoption meant that a family would love me forever and help to give me a new life, what if I let them down?"

Her shoulders sag as she grips onto the box. "Exactly," she exhales. "I don't want Carly to be disappointed in whoever I eventually become. I want to make her proud. Make her not regret taking a chance on me."

She opens the lid and uncovers my necklace that Sharon had once given me. I pick it up from the box and move her hair from her shoulders so that I can clasp the piece of jewelry around her neck.

"This necklace was a gift from one of my foster parents on the day I was leaving her house. We remained close, her son even saved my life once, but I was never adopted by her. She gave me this to remember that no matter where I landed, no matter what direction life took me, there were people who loved me and to not lose myself in the journey."

As soon as the necklace is in place, I turn her to face me once again. "You see, Leah, life is going to be filled with good and bad, proud moments as well as times of disappointment. Carly is taking a step on this journey knowing that. So yes, the world that you know is ending but the journey toward a new beginning is within your grasp."

She grips onto the pendant, just as I had once done, evoking the emotion of a time I have worked to forget. "Let this necklace be a reminder that the path will be filled with uncertainty and hard times, but that nothing you have or will experience will diminish the love that this family has for you."

Leah smiles and wraps her arms around me. "Thank you, Campbell."

"It's time, it's time," Liv exclaims, rushing up to us and tugging on the hem of Leah's dress. "It's our turn to make you my sister!" Liv jumps up and down with excitement, and Carly follows behind her, placing her hands on Liv's shoulders to calm her down.

Carly stretches her hand out to Leah and smiles brightly at her. "It's our turn. Are you ready to make it official?" she asks.

Leah looks to me momentarily before accepting Carly's hand and standing up next to her. She takes a deep breath, adjusts her dress one last time, and takes a step toward the courtroom.

I watch as Leah takes Olivia's hand in hers, and with a look of confidence and determination announces, "I'm ready."

Epilogue

Vivian

I don't think our lives are anything like we expected.

Heartache, heartbreak, happiness, friendship, love, loss, we have experienced them all, but somehow our stories of ruin have found hope. Jen, Campbell, and Carly, they are the family I choose for myself, and I am the family they chose.

Will always told me that a love worth fighting for is a love worth waiting for. He was a man I fought for, and Brooks is the man I waited for. The love our group will celebrate today is both.

"Jen is freaking out. You have got to get in there and talk her off the cliff," Campbell says, peeking her head into the bathroom.

I finish washing my hands and grab a towel to dry them, being extra careful not to wrinkle my satin dress. "Get that woman a shot. She told him she would do this, she has to follow through. Everyone is here already."

"Yeah, I'll let you tell her that," Cam adds before leaving as quickly as she appeared.

I grab my flowers off the countertop and open the door to the main hallway. My heels click against the hardwood as I move closer to the bedroom, unfortunately the profanity gets louder the closer I get as well.

"Son of a fucking bitch," I hear Jen shout. "How in the hell am I supposed to do this?"

I quickly open the door and shut it behind me to prevent anyone else from hearing her rant.

As soon as she hears the click of the lock, Jen turns to me panicked. "I don't think I can do this. This needs to be perfect."

I walk around her to peer over her shoulder. "Yes you can. You made a promise and you are a woman of your word. This will be so special, and I truly believe in you."

My words seem to calm her down, but a knock on the door sends Jen back into a spastic tizzy.

"Jen, are you ready?" Royce asks from the other side of the door.

Her eyes pop out of her head and she begins to scramble from table to table. "Stall!" she says in a frantic whisper.

I wave her away and crack open the door. Royce stands before me, his tux is crisp, his shaggy hair cut short for the occasion and his goatee trimmed to perfection.

"She needs just a few more minutes. She's putting a few more final touches on everything,"

He looks down at his watch and frowns. I don't blame him, Jen should have had everything ready weeks ago, but she waited until the last minute.

"It's ready," she shouts from behind me, and Royce noticeably relaxes. I open the door the rest of the way and Jen hands him the gift that she has been so feverishly assembling.

He places his card on top and grins at both of us. "Thank you so much, Jen," he says.

"Are we square?" she asks, adjusting her dress.

"You bet your ass," he tells her, tucking the present under his arm, turning, and heading toward the room Carly is in.

Jen and I follow close behind and are soon joined by Campbell who went in search of a tequila shot for Jen. Cam hands it to her and Jen slams it mid-stride.

"Thanks, I fucking needed that," she whispers to her.

We don't want to interrupt Royce's moment, but we sure as hell aren't going to miss it either, so we follow close on his heels. We all soon reach her door, and Royce knocks.

"It's me, pink. I have something for you," he says.

"We're out here, too," Jen hollers. Everyone looks at her and scowls. "What? We are."

She cracks open the door, and reaches her hand through. Royce laces his fingers through hers and brings her hand to his mouth. When he plants a soft kiss on her knuckles, my stomach flutters with an anxious excitement for these two people, for my family that I love so dearly.

"Don't forget to read the card," he says before kissing her hand one last time, handing me the present, and walking down the hall toward the backyard.

As soon as he's out of view, we give her the all clear and she opens the door. We all rush in and I hand her the gift-wrapped box.

The three of us circle around her as she opens the lid to the box. Inside there are two Ping-Pong balls and the project that Jen had been working on. She picks the balls up and laughs, apparently at some inside joke she never mentioned to us.

She then pulls the album out of the box and opens the front cover. Tears spring to her eyes as she slowly flips from page to page. Finally, when she share its contents with us, it becomes clear why Jen struggled with its completion and Carly's emotion, because I too battle my own tears. We are silent, only sniffles filling the void as we see each page.

Embossed across the cover is the simple phrase: Love is where you are.

Every page is filled with photos of Carly with each of us, with her daughters, with Royce, special moments that Jen captured over that last couple of years. An entire section is left blank in the back, and it reads: Where our story continues.

I rush to get tissues and hand her one to dab her eyes.

"You made this, Jen?" Carly asks, wiping her tears away.

"Royce asked me to put it together for you," Jen explains. "He supervised every damn picture that went into it. I've worked with some demanding people, and that man took the cake. He wanted it perfect."

"It is," she says, gripping onto the book and holding it close to her chest.

"The card! Don't forget the card," Campbell interrupts. Her swelling belly is something I never thought I would see. Jen threw a King Kong style temper tantrum when she had to find a maternity bridesmaid dress for her, but Campbell looks gorgeous. Lakin has doted on her like nothing I've ever seen. He is so excited to finally meet his son and daughter.

"Crap!" Carly exclaims, finding the lid and pulling the card from the paper. She moves her fingers under the seal and takes out the card to read aloud.

PINK,

I'M SO GLAD I FOUND ENOUGH BALLS TO ASK YOU TO MARRY ME.

LOVE,

ROYCE

P.S. THANK YOU FOR SAYING YES.

The End

www.ingramcontent.com/pod-product-compliance
Lightning Source LLC
Chambersburg PA
CBHW031959170626
46807CB00006B/2561